ON THE FLOOR NEAR ████████████████████, ALMOST UNNOTICED IN THE GLOOM, WAS A PLAYING CARD. SOLITAIRE, BUFFY THOUGHT BITTERLY.

"He came here to fight you," she said softly.

"I'm a vampire, remember. I heal fast. I'll be fine. Soon." He rubbed a spot on his neck that was raw, wincing at the flare of pain. "Besides, it's night now. He's lost his advantage. But he's coming for you next."

"So it really is true," Buffy said. "He's . . . immune to the sun."

"Definitely," Angel responded. He composed himself, walking in slow circles to test his bruised and burnt legs. "I'd heard rumors about a day-walking vampire, hundreds of years ago, but I never believed it. Vampires don't just walk around in the sunlight. I thought it was an urban legend."

"To scare the little vampire children?" Buffy said, but Angel wasn't smiling at her attempt at humor. "All the Watcher books and journals can't be wrong, can they?"

Angel shook his head. Images of Solitaire blithely walking through shafts of direct sunlight haunted him. "Whatever he is, he's dangerous."

Buffy the Vampire Slayer™

Available from ARCHWAY Paperbacks and POCKET PULSE

Buffy the Vampire Slayer adult books

Available from POCKET BOOKS

BUFFY
THE VAMPIRE
SLAYER™

GHOUL TROUBLE

John Passarella

An original novel based on the hit TV series created by Joss Whedon

POCKET PULSE

New York   London   Toronto   Sydney   Singapore

Historian's Note:
This story takes place during
the third season of Buffy.

An Original Publication of POCKET BOOKS

 A Pocket Pulse, published by
POCKET BOOKS, a division of Simon & Schuster, Inc.
1230 Avenue of the Americas, New York, NY 10020

™ and copyright © 2000 by Twentieth Century Fox Film
Corporation. All rights reserved.

ISBN: 0-7434-0042-9

First Pocket Books printing October 2000

10 9 8 7 6 5 4 3 2

POCKET PULSE and colophon are registered
trademarks of Simon & Schuster, Inc.

Printed in the U.S.A.

For
Gloria Wagner,
who fought a private battle against the forces of darkness
with the courage of a Slayer
and the faith of a Watcher . . .
called too soon to conduct a choir of angels.

ACKNOWLEDGMENTS

My thanks to Kara Wagner and Andrea,
for their early encouragement,

Lisa Clancy, my editor,
for warning me early on about the whip,

Gordon Kato, my agent, who is probably wondering
what he's gotten himself into,

and my parents, for their Saturdays on the road.

GHOUL TROUBLE

PROLOGUE

Not too far behind him, the water lapped against the docks of Sunnydale's seedy waterfront district. Just ahead was the yellow neon sign of the EZ Rider Saloon, basically a biker bar. About a dozen motorcycles, glinting chrome in abundance, were lined up with something approaching military precision on the gravel parking lot. The saloon itself had been haphazardly built from cinderblocks and plywood, the former painted black, the latter a sickening shade of green. Various neon beer logos adorned each small window. All the buzzing neon sounded like a swarm of irritated wasps.

Solitaire walked in long, easy strides, his black overcoat fluttering back from his black shirt and pants, revealing a red leather vest. A minor affectation dating back hundreds of years, he dressed in red and black to represent the colors of the suits in a deck of playing cards. His black boots fell softly on the concrete as he took the steps two at a time and swung open the front door of the saloon.

Through the smoky haze of the dimly lit saloon, Solitaire counted thirteen hard-edged bikers. *Many humans consider thirteen an unlucky number,* he thought. *Maybe they have good cause.* He chuckled softly, rubbing his hands together with a degree of anticipation he hadn't felt in over a century. He'd sorely missed the competition of his duels, but the pool of worthy opponents had been uninspiring. *Until now.* Here, in Sunnydale, he finally expected to find a foe worthy of his skills. Yet after such a long period of unfocused destruction—*going through the motions, really*—he was not foolish enough to believe he was in top form. Human pugilists, boxers, honed their skills on sparring partners and Solitaire wasn't above a little sparring of his own to get into fighting trim. *Well, let's call a spade a spade,* he thought, appropriately enough, considering his chosen name. *Killing trim.*

His gaze swept the group, seeking his target while assessing what would soon become the arena for the match. Most of the bikers ambled around the three pool tables, alternately drinking from tall-necked beer bottles and sinking balls in called pockets. Many smoked cigarettes, but a few puffed on cheap cigars wedged into the corners of their mouths. Whether their jackets were leather or denim, the backs of every one were embroidered with the image of a flaming skull. Solitaire had a hunch the gang's logo would prove prophetic this night.

A lone bartender was on duty, cleaning glasses with a

dingy rag behind a narrow bar, almost a counter. From an outdated jukebox in the corner opposite the door blared the Blue Oyster Cult song, "Don't Fear the Reaper." *Again,* Solitaire thought, *a prophetic choice for musical accompaniment.*

In the far back corner of the EZ Rider Saloon, sitting on a tall four-legged stool with one elbow resting on a windowsill, was a barrel-chested biker with heavy arms wearing an unbuttoned black leather vest. His other hand gripped the handle of a large mug of beer that rested on his hairy stomach. Next to him stood a wiry man whose skin was the color and texture of rawhide. His boots actually sported real spurs. As he related a story that culminated in a rudely suggestive motion of his hips, the big man gave a hearty laugh, causing his beer to slosh back and forth in the glass. Foam lapped over the edge and settled on his hairy gut, not that the big biker gave it more than passing notice.

Solitaire approached the nearest biker and, just as the man was about to sink the nine ball in the corner pocket, said, "I'm looking for Warhammer."

The man had a long knife scar along his cheek, pointing toward a permanently squinted right eye. Stitched over the chest pocket of his threadbare denim jacket was the name CYCLOPS. Solitaire figured the right eye was glass. "Buzz off," Cyclops said and belched for good measure. As a heavy biker on the opposite side of the table chuckled over the rude dismissal, Cyclops bent over his shot again. He winked at his beefy partner with his good eye and said, "Gotta put these town clowns in their place, Hef."

3

Solitaire snatched the pool cue out of Cyclops's hands and whipped it around behind his legs, spilling the one-eyed biker to the plywood floor with a loud grunt and a louder curse.

Hef rushed around the table. "Hey! What the—?" He never finished the sentence, so quickly had Solitaire rammed the butt of the pool cue into his flabby gut. Doubled over in pain, Hef was ill-prepared to offer further protest.

The bartender yelled, "Hey, buddy, you're asking for big trouble. Get lost or you'll need an ambulance."

Solitaire turned and hurled the pool cue like a spear, aiming high. The bartender screamed and dropped to the floor as the grimy mirror behind him shattered into a thousand pieces.

Solitaire never saw his own reflection.

Boot spurs jangling, the rawhide-skinned biker strode across the length of the bar with a cowboy swagger. Solitaire almost had to laugh but that would have spoiled the moment. Rawhide stopped two feet from Solitaire and whipped out a switchblade, which he pointed at Solitaire's throat.

"Where are your shooting irons, cowboy?" Solitaire asked.

"Name's Loon," the man said. "Wanna know why they call me Loon? 'Cause I'm just crazy enough to carve your face up like a Christmas ham. Care to explain your death wish before I commence my wet work?"

"I'm here for Warhammer," Solitaire said. "The rest of you may live." Solitaire was aware of Cyclops and Hef casually sidling up on either side of him, probably intending to pull his arms back so Loon would have an easy time with his switchblade.

The barrel-chested biker, who had been perched on the stool with a mug of beer on his hairy belly, called out, "I'm Warhammer. What makes you think I want to waste my time kicking the spit out of your sorry carcass?"

"Fear is a perfectly natural response," Solitaire said, grinning.

That hearty laugh again, shaking the thick stomach. "Hardly," Warhammer said. "You want your shot at me? Work your way through these . . . *gentlemen* first."

Several of them laughed at the term.

"My pleasure."

"Yeah, right," Warhammer said after a moment, nodding his head. "You're a bigger fool than I took you for." Warhammer spread his hands magnanimously. "Just realize there won't be enough of you left for me to scrape off my boot heel."

Loon smiled with a slight nod to the biker Solitaire knew was standing behind his left side. Solitaire didn't have to see the man. He could smell his beer breath, hear the quickened beat of his heart. When Loon lunged forward with his switchblade, Solitaire caught Loon's wrist in his left hand and squeezed hard, hearing bones crunch. He planted his right hand on Loon's shoulder and used the man's own momentum to pull him forward. The extended knife blade drove hilt-deep into Cyclops's good eye. *Well*, thought Solitaire, *"good" was all a matter of semantics now*. Loon released the knife, screaming from the pain of his ruined wrist. Cyclops simply fell with a thud, the knife lodged deep in his brain.

Hef charged from the other side and wrapped his meaty hands around Solitaire's neck, intending to throttle. Solitaire peeled back one of Hef's fingers until it snapped, then popped a second and a third until, finally, Hef realized he was rapidly running out of functioning fingers and let go. Without even turning around, Solitaire drove his elbow into the man's face, driving nose cartilage back into his skull. Another body fell to the floor.

A fourth biker came thundering across the nearest pool table, knocking aside the hanging, green-shaded light as he dove toward Solitaire. Catching the airborne biker by the throat and belt buckle, Solitaire increased his elevation, flipping him into the jukebox. Varicolored glass shattered and the music screeched to a halt, replaced by the sizzle and hiss of sparks. The biker's face was a bloody ruin.

Four down, eight to go before Warhammer. He wondered if they had the stomach for it. Then again, one required a modicum of intelligence to know when to retreat, so Solitaire figured they would all be around until the bitter end. Warhammer himself had hopped down from his stool, his smirk of casual disregard replaced by, if not concern, a new measure of respect. *Good,* Solitaire thought. *I finally have his attention.*

Two more bikers came at Solitaire from opposite sides, each holding a pool cue like a baseball bat. Solitaire waited until the first one yelled "Batter up," and swung for the fences. Solitaire's forearm caught the brunt of the pool cue, splitting it cleanly in half. At the same moment he leaned sideways and fired a kick into the other biker's gut before he could begin his swing. He slammed into the wall and fell over, clutching a half-dozen shattered ribs. Solitaire turned to the man still holding half a pool cue and twisted his arm up behind his back until the arm dislocated from the shoulder. He then bent the man over and shoved him headfirst into the wall.

Just as Solitaire straightened up, he saw the blur of a steel-toed boot driving directly toward his crotch. His reflexes were faster than the kick. Catching the boot in both hands, he wrenched the man's foot with enough torque to shatter the ankle. The biker fell, writhing on his back as he screamed in pain. "Make it stop! Please! Please—make it stop!" As much as Solitaire enjoyed the man's pain, the yowling was a bit much on his ears. He launched his own kick, but his landed with a sickening thud, rupturing the man's temple. "All better now," Solitaire remarked.

Another biker charged, yelling, "You killed Spud!" He swung a beer bottle at Solitaire's head, but Solitaire ducked under the blow, caught the man around the waist and flipped him over, slamming his back down hard against the edge of a pool table, breaking his spine.

The next one was called Viper. He slipped on a pair of brass knuckles, with sharp metal spikes sticking out from each ring. "Had these custom-made," he explained. "Like to grind my own hamburger." He barreled forward with a yell, both spiked fists flying. Solitaire pulled a pool cue from a wall rack and jabbed the pointed end right into the man's solar plexus. As Viper staggered back, Solitaire swung the cue stick around in a great whistling arc. It shattered across the bridge of the man's nose. Viper went down, moaning in agony.

Solitaire picked up the white cue ball and the black

eight ball. He fired the cue ball with major-league speed at the nearest biker's head, smashing his nose. Then the eight ball shattered another man's front teeth. He sputtered and howled in pain, strands of bloody drool webbing down from his greasy fingers. An easy spin kick to the head took him down and put him out of his misery.

One last man stood between Solitaire and Warhammer. This one was tall, but stood hunched over, emphasizing a hooked nose and a paunch that hung over his large silver belt buckle in the shape of the state of Texas. His name patch read HAWK. He seemed too confident. In a moment, Solitaire knew why. The man pulled a .357 revolver out of a shoulder holster, grinning like a magician who has just produced a bouquet of flowers from the sleeve of his tuxedo. He pointed his arm straight out, the wide bore of the barrel level with Solitaire's chest. "Game over, man!"

Almost as if time had slowed down, Solitaire saw the trigger finger tense. His own hands moved with lightning speed. His right hand chopped down on the inside of Hawk's elbow just as his left hand went under Hawk's wrist, jackknifing the man's forearm, directing the barrel of the gun up, up, as the trigger finger continued to squeeze. The barrel was under Hawk's chin when the Magnum went off, splattering the wall with what passed for Hawk's brains.

Hawk slumped to the ground.

"Fear is a perfectly natural response," Solitaire told Warhammer for the second time.

All around him lay a dozen men, some dead, some

dying and the rest in desperate need of medical attention, a weak chorus of sobs and moans an audible testament to that fact. "I don't scare easy," Warhammer replied, demonstrating his own lack of brains.

He was as tall as Solitaire, but much thicker through the chest and upper arms, with layers of muscle only slightly gone to seed. "Catch," he said, throwing the half-filled mug of beer at Solitaire's head.

Solitaire swatted the mug aside, expecting the heavier man to bull rush him, but was surprised when Warhammer reached back and hoisted the barstool up by two of its legs. He brought it down quickly, hoping to crush Solitaire's skull with one mighty blow, a tactic that had probably earned the biker his nickname. But Solitaire ducked nimbly to the right, then snap-kicked the outside of Warhammer's left knee, hyperextending it inward.

Warhammer roared in pain but launched a roundhouse right. Off balance, he missed high and wide, allowing Solitaire to duck inside and land a crushing blow to Warhammer's right kidney. The biker crumpled to his knees, but managed to wrap both arms around Solitaire's calves and flip him backward. The back of Solitaire's head rapped against the edge of the pool table as he fell, causing him to wince as the lights blinked out for an instant.

But a moment was enough time for Warhammer to use his weight advantage. He straddled Solitaire's prostrate form and wrapped beefy hands around his throat. For the first time, Solitaire needed a distraction to recover from a vulnerable position. The transformation was instantaneous. His face contorted, his eyes burned yellow and slavering fangs appeared under snarling lips.

Warhammer froze, his jaw dropping. "What the—?"

Solitaire was quick to seize the advantage. Clasping his hands together, he swung them up with enough force to break Warhammer's grip. He then struck the biker under the chin with the heel of his right hand, slamming his jaw shut. Solitaire followed with a succession of powerful jabs, alternating left, right, left, right, until Warhammer fell back, blood streaming from his smashed nose and split cheeks. In a move that initially confused Solitaire, the big man fumbled at his pants leg until he finally pulled a hunting knife from a sheath inside his boot. Solitaire chopped at his wrist with enough force to shatter bone, and the blade clattered to the floor. Solitaire swept it aside with the back of his hand, far out of the big biker's reach.

Warhammer rolled over on his side and scrambled toward Hawk's still form, working his way toward the gun. Solitaire leapt to his feet and caught Warhammer by the scalp with his left hand, then clamped his right hand under the man's grizzled jaw. Warhammer's fingers spasmed inches from the butt of the gun until the vicious twist of Solitaire's arms snapped his neck.

Solitaire planted his boot heel on Warhammer's face as he reached into his red vest and removed a playing card. A king of clubs. He dropped it on the dead man's back and said, "You were highly overrated, Warhammer."

Yet that was not the whole truth. Warhammer, a mere human, had gotten the better of him, if only for a moment, and Solitaire had had to resort to a flash of fangs to regain the advantage. The duelist in him was disgusted with his own inadequacy. He could never afford such slip-ups in high stakes matches, especially in the battle to come, the one challenge that had drawn him out of his listless retirement. Cracking his knuckles, he remarked, "Definitely rusty."

As he walked back through the saloon, several of the bikers continued to writhe and moan on the floor. Not one made an effort to stop him. Those with any sense were glad to see the last of him, or would be, once the medication kicked in. Only after Solitaire strode out the door did the barman raise his head above the counter. He took a moment or two to survey the carnage, then reached for the telephone with trembling hands.

Outside the EZ Rider, Solitaire paused beside the row of motorcycles with their glistening chrome and Grateful Dead decals. He planted his foot on the seat of the first one in the line and gave a great shove. Like a row of dominoes they went down, one after the other, protesting screeches of steel that ended long before the first sirens could be heard.

Despite convincing Solitaire that his skills could use a little honing, Warhammer had been, for the most part, a disappointment. Yet it was hard to blame humans for their weaknesses. *Just so much flesh and blood and fragile bones.* Still, he was confident the Slayer would present a greater challenge. Maybe even the ultimate challenge. *Yes.* He smiled. *It's good to be back in the game.*

He left the gravel lot and started the long walk down the two-lane state road, away from the docks and into the golden sunrise. He stopped and squinted into the glare, gave a slight hiss through his fangs. Then he reached into an overcoat pocket and removed a pair of metal-rimmed aviator sunglasses. He slipped them on and sighed, then walked into the light of the new day.

CHAPTER 1

It started out like an ordinary cemetery patrol—if there was such a thing—right up till the moment the hulking vampire wearing the UC Sunnydale football jersey caught Buffy's spin kick mid-spin and pre-kick. He hurled her backward, right into the tombstone. Her head struck the side of the stone with a sickening thud and she went down hard, stunned. While Buffy was still too woozy to put up much of a fight, the vampire advanced on her with a feral glint in his yellow eyes.

Fortunately, she wasn't alone. Xander Harris moved to intercept the vampire, one of Buffy's wooden stakes clutched in his hand. Relative to the vampire's size, the stake felt more like a toothpick. "Okay, Baby Huey," Xander said. "I got something for you. Right here."

The vampire turned toward Xander, and growled in

full vampface. Out of the corner of his eye, Xander could see Willow scrambling for the crossbow the vampire had swatted out of Buffy's hands before she'd had a chance to use it. "Let's see," Xander said, backing up slightly, trying to turn the vampire away from Willow's position, "you're wearing number seventy-two, got that big ol' barrel gut . . . I'm guessing offensive lineman, big fella."

Xander had once earned a spot on the Sunnydale High swim team—around the same time half the team was turning into carnivorous fish monsters—and, even though he lacked the element of surprise, he was betting that quick-and-wiry would give him the upper hand over big-and-bulky. *Even though big bulky guy has a blood-thirsty demon riding shotgun where his soul used to be.*

Before he completely unnerved himself, Xander yelled and drove the stake toward the vampire's heart. In an eye blink, he felt his wrist caught in a crushing grip, the point of the stake inches short of the mark. The vampire laughed and hoisted him bodily into the air. "Okay," Xander said, slightly breathless. "As plans go, I have to admit that lacked in the subtlety department . . . big-time."

Around his neck, the vampire wore a crude chain from which dangled one of the little metal skulls that marked the bloodsucker as one of Skull John's crew. *No big surprise there.* The vampire's fetid breath washed over Xander. "I'll suck you dry, runt. Then the girls."

"What? No ladies first? Where's your manners . . . lard-butt?" He swung an awkward kick at the vampire's shin, with little effect.

The glistening fangs inched closer to Xander's throat.

He grimaced and said overly loudly, "Now would be a real good time for that old cavalry horn to sound."

Instead of a bugle, he heard the release of a crossbow bolt. The vampire roared and dropped Xander unceremoniously at his feet. Judging by the lack of dust factor, Xander guessed the bolt had missed the vampire's heart. A guess confirmed when the vampire whirled around to face Willow, revealing the feather-tufted end of the quarrel just below his right shoulder blade.

Willow Rosenberg backed up a step. "Oops."

The vampire was distracted by Buffy at his feet. She moaned, struggling to her hands and knees, but fell again. As the vampire Slayer, the Chosen One, she recovered faster than an ordinary person, healed from wounds incredibly fast, and could generally keep on slaying long after she'd suffered injuries severe enough to land anyone else in the emergency room. Nevertheless, she could be hurt, stunned, even killed—had been killed once, briefly, until Xander resuscitated her with CPR. She was recovering now, but not fast enough. The vampire went down on one knee beside her, bared his fangs again.

Xander was climbing to his feet, stake in hand, when Angel came charging from the opposite direction, his black duster whipping behind him. The vampire looked up, startled for a moment, before Angel's doubled fist clubbed the side of his head.

"Leave it to Dead Boy to make a dramatic entrance," Xander said softly.

"I heard that," Angel said as he drove his heel into the chest of the lineman vampire, staggering him.

"We had everything under control here, right, Will?" Xander said, looking to Willow for moral support.

"Right! We're, um, masters of control and everything," she said as she awkwardly attempted to reload the crossbow.

Angel had backed the much larger vampire against a tree. "Xander, give me that stake."

"Nothing would please me more," Xander said with a dark glint in his eye. Nonetheless he tossed the stake to Angel, who was now in full vampface, as often happened when he was in battle.

The lineman vampire charged Angel before he could bring the stake to bear. Dropping his shoulder, he bowled Angel over, no mean feat. Angel lost the stake, but rolled with the impact, driving a knee into the bulky vampire's gut and using his momentum against him. With a grunt, the vampire slammed into a leaning tombstone.

Cordelia Chase ran into the clearing, still flushed from trying to keep up with Angel. Ever fashion-conscious in a long-sleeved black V-neck sweater over a leopard-skin print skirt, she looked like she was on a date rather than out patrolling for vampires and other things that went *suck* in the night. She took one look at the vampire lineman and said, "Eeeuw!"

Xander nodded. "I hear you. Two butt-ugly vampires wrasslin' in the dirt. Disgusting."

"No," she said, "I think I used to date that guy."

"Now, I'm disgusted," Xander said. He ran toward the dropped stake. "Is there anyone you haven't dated?"

"Just seems that way, Xander Harris," she said tartly. "I hit rock bottom with you. I'm much choosier now."

"Hussy, thy name is Cordelia," Willow said innocently.

But the vampire was up, and swiping at Angel with long, meaty arms. With a roar, he rushed Angel, who stood his ground to meet the charge. Xander picked up the stake but Angel wasn't watching for it.

Buffy was back on her hands and knees. Amazingly, she burst into a sprint from that position and launched herself onto the back of the vampire lineman. She caught his heavy neck chain in her left hand and pulled back on it, closing it up in her fist to throttle him. No matter how much the chain dug into his throat, it was hardly more than an inconvenience for the vampire who, being technically dead, would never breathe again anyway. Buffy could not choke him into submission, which left her only one recourse. "Xander! Stake!"

Xander tossed it to her and she snagged it out of the air with her right hand, bringing it down into the vampire's chest with one quick motion. When the vampire exploded into a spray of dust, Buffy fell down from her lofty perch and landed . . .

. . . in Angel's arms. She brushed a strand of blond hair from her eyes and said, "We've got to stop meeting like this."

For a moment, she saw the intense longing in his eyes and was afraid it was mirrored in her own. *Don't go there,* she told herself. *There lies pain.*

"No promises," he said.

With effort, she broke away from his gaze—and his embrace. Instead, she held up the chain still clutched in her left hand. The metal skull dangled down between her fingers.

Angel nodded. "Skull John."

"Third one tonight," Buffy remarked. "I'll soon have quite the collection of morbid fashion accessories."

"Lots of Skull John goons," Xander said. "But never the big vamp himself."

Willow joined them but her attention was elsewhere. "Where's Oz?"

Cordelia looked the most startled. She shrugged. "He was right beside me."

There was a new head vampire in town, the elusive Skull John, whose vampire underlings wore the skull chain and had been running rampant of late, while Skull John himself remained a mystery. *Dust enough of his troops,* Buffy thought, *and Skull John will be forced to come out for his very own stake.* Well, it was a theory and she was sticking to it. So the Scooby Gang, sometimes known as the Slayerettes, had split into two platonic teams to patrol. Willow and Xander with Buffy on one team, with Angel, Cordelia and Oz on the other. Fewer distractions that way . . . distractions in the form of actual smoochies or thinking about potential smoochies. Though Xander and Cordelia were not about to get up close and personal anytime soon, it was still a good idea to keep the two of them apart. All business and slayage, but now one of their own was missing.

Oz had been right behind Cordelia until he noticed something gleaming in the moonlight under a bush to his right. After a careful examination, he stooped and picked it up. "Interesting," he said, then hurried to join the others.

In his haste he failed to notice a dark-cloaked woman with wild red hair crouched inhumanly still on the other side of the iron cemetery fence. When Oz moved off with his discovery, she shadowed his progress, staying low and moving quietly, darting from tree to tree.

So intent was she on Oz's movement that she almost ran into another dark-cloaked woman coming along the fence from the opposite direction. This one had a long, white Mohawk haircut that flowed into the semblance of a ponytail. She caught the redhead by her upper arm and cautioned her to silence. In her other hand she clutched a battered leather satchel. "Did you see him?" whispered the redhead.

"That's not all I saw," said the other woman. "Let's get out of here. I'll explain later."

"Oz!" Willow called, a note of alarm entering her voice.

"You rang?" Oz said casually as he stepped up beside her.

"Oh!" Willow gasped, almost jumping out of her skin. "I mean, 'Oh, there you are!' Or, 'Where were you?' As in, we were all worried. Weren't we all?"

The others nodded.

"Guys, I have some bad news," Oz said in his usual mellow tone. Only his eyes gave away his concern.

"Usually your bad news comes gift-wrapped in fur around the full moon," Xander said.

Oz quirked a smile. For three days—rather, three nights—out of the month, Oz was a werewolf. The rest of the month he was a cool, laid back kind of guy who dated Willow and played lead guitar for a band called Dingoes Ate My Baby. But now he looked worried.

"What is it, Oz?" Buffy asked.

"This," Oz said and held it up before them.

"What is it?" Cordelia asked. "I mean, besides the obvious."

Not until the next morning in the Sunnydale High School library did they learn the answer. "If I'm not mistaken," Rupert Giles, school librarian and Buffy's official Watcher, said as he absently pushed up his eyeglasses, "that would be a femur."

"One of those cute, fuzzy little monkeys at the zoo?" Xander asked.

"Femur, Xander," Giles corrected. "Not a lemur."

"Oh, so you're saying lady monkey?"

"An adult human leg bone, and rather . . . gnawed, it would seem."

"Gnawed?" Cordelia's lip curled in disgust. "Like eaten?"

"Can't get enough of that Colonel's Secret Recipe," Xander said.

Giles came out from behind the library's checkout counter, holding the bone in one hand, running the other thoughtfully through his unruly hair. He looked to Oz. "You say you found this in the cemetery?"

Oz nodded. "Under a bush. Near the fence."

Giles turned to Buffy. "And you noticed no freshly disturbed graves?" Buffy shook her head. "I suppose it's possible whatever did this just tossed the bone over the fence. It wouldn't appear to be the work of a vampire."

"Angel didn't think so," Buffy said. Angel was the only member of the patrol absent from the library. As a vampire—a vampire cursed with a soul and so, a conscience, but a vampire nonetheless—Angel had to avoid the light of day. While they were taking classes and conferring with Giles, Angel was probably deep in vamp sleep in his mansion.

"So what are we talking about?" Xander asked. "Seeing as how Sunnydale is sitting on top of the Hellmouth, we've got a whole lot of nasty options." The original Spanish settlers knew Sunnydale by a different name, *Boca del Infierno,* or Hellmouth, and for good reason. Giles had once called it "a center of mystical energy" that attracted all the demons and bogeymen that children are routinely taught not to believe in.

"Well, this doesn't appear to be the work of hellhounds," Giles said. "Hellhounds are rather savage. This bone is in excellent condition."

Willow frowned. "Not as excellent as if, oh, the owner were still attached to it and yelling, 'Ouch, my leg hurts.' "

"Um, quite," Giles said. "I believe we're looking at the handiwork of a demon with cannibalistic tendencies."

"Unlike your garden-variety, soul-sucking demon," Xander said.

"If you discount the severe scoring of the fangs," Giles said, "there's almost a gourmet delicacy about the complete consumption of the flesh and tissue, even going so far as to suck out the marrow."

Cordelia shivered. "Can I be the first to say 'Yuck!'?"

"I've got 'Ick!' covered," Willow added.

"Can Geraldo be far behind with a cafeteria food exposé?" Xander said. "My God, what have they been feeding us?"

"Xander, please," Giles said.

"Oh, right," Xander said, "you Brits and your meat pie. I see where this is going."

"Xander," Buffy said, then looked to Giles. "You're thinking, what? Zombies? Ghouls?"

"Quite possibly," Giles said, laying the bone down on the table.

"I've seen *Night of the Living Dead* oh, maybe a dozen times, so I'm all clear on the eating habits of zombies," Xander said. "But ghouls are like ghosts or poltergeists, right? Rattle chains, knock on walls in the middle of the night, and screw up cable television reception."

"Despite the similarity in the spelling of their names, ghouls are definitely unrelated to ghosts," Giles explained. "Ghouls are very much physical entities, demons in their own right. As I recall, they are discussed in Arabic folklore as being deceitful and rather fond of the taste of human flesh. But I'll need to research further."

"Deceitful, demon flesh-eaters," Xander noted. "That equals *bad guy* in my book."

Giles moved on. "Willow, could you search for reports of missing persons in the area? It's quite possible that our flesh-eaters have been operating in the area for quite a while and that we've only now discovered their presence. We need to know the extent of this problem."

"You know me," Willow said, "any excuse to go all cyber and punky."

"You make 'cyber' cute," Oz said.

Willow smiled and sat down in front of the library computer. With a rapid-fire clicking of keys, she began her on-line searches. Giles had come to tolerate and appreciate, if not understand, this one example of modern information technology in the midst of his dusty stacks and old tomes. Before the late Jenny Calendar, a devout techno-pagan, had come into his life, Giles distrusted any scrap of knowledge gleaned electronically. In his old-fashioned—some would say antiquated—view, anything important should have been committed to paper.

"Giles," Buffy said, "aren't you forgetting something?"

"Am I?"

She nodded. "People tend to go milk carton all the time in Sunnydale."

"For all sorts of Hellmouthian reasons," Xander added.

Giles frowned. "I see your point. Willow, perhaps you should narrow your search to discoveries of human remains, bones. Bare bones specifically." He turned back to Buffy. "Zombies and ghouls have been known to travel in packs. I want you to be on your guard at all times."

"That's me, twenty-four seven, on-guard girl," Buffy said, smiling to ease his concern. "Don't worry, Giles." But it was obvious from his expression that he did worry about her, all the time. She was the Slayer and he was her Watcher. He knew that Slayers were neither immortal nor invulnerable and Buffy had only become the Chosen One when her predecessor had met an untimely end. For Slayers, all endings were untimely and there were no gold watches or retirement plans. Slayers tended to die young, most never living beyond their twenties. Only Buffy's mother worried about her more than Giles did, especially since Buffy had been forced to tell her mother she was the Slayer and all that that entailed.

"Even so," Giles said. "I forbid you to patrol alone until we know exactly what we are dealing with."

Buffy's left eyebrow had gone up at the mention of the word "forbid," and it was still hanging high. And Giles was aware of it then and now.

"All right then, I strongly *advise* you to patrol in pairs or groups."

Their working relationship had often involved Buffy breaking the typical Slayer rules and Giles had been forced to admit, begrudgingly at times, that her methods were often effective. As such, she'd received more leeway from her Watcher than any Slayer before her, a fact that often landed Giles in hot water with the Watchers Council back in England.

Buffy smiled. "Much better, Giles."

"Please, *do* be careful," Giles saw fit to add, making another slight adjustment to his glasses.

"Before I forget," Buffy said. "Picked up some more trinkets last night." She upended a brown paper bag she had brought to school and three chains with three little skulls spilled out on the counter.

Giles gathered them up, frowning. "Skull John. This makes over a dozen of his followers that you've slain."

"Not that I'm counting, but it's fourteen."

"This was to be expected. Spike's departure created a void in the vampire leadership in Sunnydale. And nature abhors a vacuum."

"As do the forces of evil, apparently," Xander commented.

"Skull John's a skulker," Buffy said, seeing a connection. "Could he be responsible for the bone we found?"

Giles shook his head. "Aside from his gruesome fascination with skulls, he is a vampire and a vampire's interest in human anatomy rarely extends beyond an unquenchable thirst for blood."

"Noted. Skull John not a flesh-eater suspect. But I still have a stake with his name carved on it."

The first class bell rang.

"Drudgery calls," Buffy said, and trudged out of the library.

CHAPTER 2

"Riding a horse across the green hills of Ireland, with a medieval castle in the distance, rising out of the morning mist. One of those really old ones with a moat and everything," Willow said wistfully.

"Good one, Will," Buffy said, then closed her eyes and thought for a moment. "Maui," she said, rolling the word over her tongue to savor the exotic sound of it. They were sitting on a bench in the school courtyard during a shared study period, playing the spring break version of Anywhere but Here. "I'm lying on a beach in Maui, sipping one of those drinks with an umbrella in it, as the sun rises."

"Hawaii, yes—ooh, but wait, if it's morning then Angel couldn't be there with you to sip those umbrella thingies, since the sun would be burning him to ashes."

"Right," Buffy conceded with a brief grimace. "Exchange one sunrise for a sunset and Angel shows up a little late. I think it's a plan."

"A good plan."

The class bell rang and was followed by a rush of students. Moments later Oz walked up to Willow's end of the bench, placed a foot on the edge of the seat and balanced his books on his knee. "Hey," he said to Willow.

"Hey, you."

Xander approached from the opposite direction, slipping free of the stream of students. "What's the what?"

"We were talking about where we'd like to go for spring break," Willow said. "The Anywhere but Here edition which, as you know, makes money not an object."

"I could definitely use some quality time in a hyperbaric chamber," Oz said. Off Willow's frown, he added, "But, one of those cozy two-seater models."

"Fort Lauderdale or Daytona Beach," Xander said, his gaze drifting into the distance. "Ah, hard to beat the classics."

"And visions of bikini-clad supermodels danced in his head," Buffy remarked. "A shining example of the typical adolescent male's one-track mind."

"Who said anything about bikinis?" Xander said, then quickly added, "But why the daydreams anyway? General principles?"

Willow shook her head. "I was assigned a term paper today for A.P. History. Lottery topics. We lose a whole grade level if we switch."

"No big, Will," Xander said. "You can ace any topic."

"That's the problem," Buffy said.

"What?" asked Oz, puzzled.

Willow sighed. "My topic is the history of Sunnydale, from Spanish settlement to present day."

"Okay, as topics go it's a little broad," Xander said. "But Sunnydale's a little burg. What's the problem?"

"She's a little undecided," Buffy said.

"About?"

Willow said, "Should I use the term 'Hellmouth' in my thesis statement or save it for the big conclusion."

Oz grinned mischievously. "Be bold. Go with the thesis statement."

"Oz!" Willow said.

Xander frowned. "I see," he said. "That would be taking the devil's advocate position a little too literally."

"Somehow it's a bad thing to know too much," Oz said. "Incredible."

"Exactly," Willow said. "Therefore we have no choice but to daydream ourselves many time zones from here."

"Fall on the grenade, Will," Xander said. "Take the B. Over the years I've learned it doesn't make all that much difference to my folks if I bring home B's or D's. If it's not a complication in their lives, it's not a problem."

"Remember my midterm physics grade?" Oz asked. "Identical to last year's." He shook his head. "It's a whole space–time continuum thing. Take what you can get."

Meaning I should switch topics and take the lower grade. "I don't want to just give up . . . or lie," Willow replied. "That would be like cheating."

"I have just the thing to take your mind off the ethical issues of the day," Xander said and removed a flyer from one of his notebooks. "Have you guys seen this? New band at the Bronze. Special engagement, five nights only. Interested?"

Buffy pulled the flyer out of his hand, examining the grainy, black and white photocopied image of the band under the name Vyxn. "Xander, this is an all-girl group wearing leather . . . well, actually, not all that much leather."

"I, for one, support women in rock," Xander said defensively. "Besides, they're supposed to be good. I hear they wowed 'em at UC Sunnydale."

Oz glanced at the flyer. "Interesting."

Good old Oz, Buffy thought. *I can't tell if he's curious or jealous.*

"Should be tons of fun," Xander said. "What do you say?"

"Miss Summers," a woman called in an excited voice.

They all looked up as a dark-haired woman approached, carrying a stack of folders with various slips of paper protruding from them. She looked one stiff wind away from organizational disaster. "Glad I finally caught up with you."

"This can't be good," Xander whispered to Oz.

Willow looked a question at Buffy, who gave a slight shrug of ignorance. "Just sitting here basking," Buffy said to the woman, smiling. When one faced ravenous vampires by night, a disorganized administrator type in the light of day was not all that terrifying. *Well, mostly.* Principal Snyder did have his oogie moments. "I don't believe we've met."

"I'm Carole Burzak," the woman said. "Mrs. Burzak. Your new guidance counselor. Could I have a few moments with you, in private? This is a matter of grave concern for your future."

Buffy hopped off the bench, gave the others a slightly unsettled look before taking a few steps away with her guidance counselor. "My future?"

"Exactly," Mrs. Burzak said. "In my opinion, there's too much seizing the day going on and not enough stockpiling of nuts."

"Excuse me?"

"I'm concerned about your red zones, Miss Summers," Mrs. Burzak said, abandoning mixed metaphors for something entirely cryptic. "I reviewed your class standings and performance and I've identified two yellow zones and a red zone. I'm afraid if you do not address these zones immediately you will jeopardize your future."

"Yellow zones? Red zones? Would this have anything to do with football, because I'm not even on the cheerleading squad—"

"Schoolwork, Miss Summers. They have everything to do with schoolwork. It's a system I've developed."

"The Burzak system?"

"I measure the occurrences of absences and tardies, the progression of exam scores and term paper grades. Young lady, you are in danger of failing three courses: English, Math and History. Fail the courses, repeat the year, and forget about college. You were planning on college next year, weren't you?" She rifled through her folders before Buffy could form a reply. "Ah, yes. Right here. University of California at Sunnydale."

"Thanks for caring," Buffy tried, "about all my . . . zones and everything."

"Don't take this lightly, Miss Summers," Mrs. Burzak said. "One gets very few second chances in life. I advise you to address your trouble zones immediately and, if I were you" —she plucked the Vyxn flyer out of Buffy's hands and gave it a quick, dismissive review before handing it back—"I would start spending my evenings with books instead of bands."

"Books good," Buffy said with a nod. "Bands bad. Got it."

Mrs. Burzak stared her down for a moment or two. "Miss Summers. *Buffy.* I want you to know I never give up on a student, even if she gives up on herself."

"That's, um . . . comforting."

"I consider these yellow and red zones as much my responsibility as yours. We're a team. We'll get all your zones green again in time for graduation. That's a Burzak promise!" She patted her burgeoning folders into a semblance of order, gave a brisk nod of encouragement and walked away.

Buffy walked back to the others, feeling a little numb.

"That was—" Xander began.

"We couldn't help but hear about all your zones and stuff," Willow said.

"She wants all my zones green again," Buffy said pertly.

Oz nodded sympathetically. "It's not easy being green."

The sandwich board sign outside the Bronze announced the SPECIAL ENGAGEMENT—5 NIGHTS ONLY appearance of Vyxn. In the center of the sign, tilted at a slight angle, was a much larger version of the band's publicity still. Four extremely attractive women with im-

31

probably wild hairstyles, clad in just enough strips and triangles of leather to avoid arrest under any state indecency laws. Dramatic applications of makeup emphasized their various come-hither and pouty expressions.

"Tacky," Buffy said.

"Tasteless," Willow said.

"Cool," Xander said. "I wonder if they'll sell posters after the show."

"We're not staying *after* the show," Buffy reminded him. "Remember: one set. That was the deal. This feels very . . . red zone-y to me."

"Well, we brought our books," Willow said, hefting her backpack for emphasis. "That's a good thing. A little music, a little patrolling followed by a little studying."

"All part of a Slayer's well-balanced day," Xander said.

The Bronze made no pretense to exclusivity. Everyone was welcome, which in no way dampened the amount of business on any given night, for the simple reason that the Bronze had little or no competition in Sunnydale. For those of legal drinking age, alcohol was available.

The warmup act played as if they had sleepwalked on stage and only vaguely recalled how to play their instruments. In keeping with the somnambulistic theme, the lead singer kept his eyes closed while he sang his lyrics in a whispered monotone. A round of polite applause died out before they had even left the stage.

Buffy, Willow and Oz sat at a table stacked with unopened textbooks. Xander sat alone on a sofa closer to the stage, impatiently awaiting the arrival of Vyxn.

Cordelia was nowhere around, no doubt hoping to restore her social status by minimizing her contact with Xander and the rest of the Scooby Gang. However, when the lights dimmed and smoke billowed out from machines positioned on either side of the stage, he sat up straighter on the sofa and thought more about Vyxn's imminent arrival than his former relationship with Queen C.

Red lights came on and the smoke diffused. The band was standing there, still as statues, as if sculptured from the smoke.

The lead singer had an unruly mop of black hair, shaved on the sides, a microphone held low, almost carelessly, in her hand. A spiky-haired brunette wearing a spiked leather collar was the drummer. Flanking the drummer was the bass player, who had wild red hair and thick eyeliner, and the lead guitarist, who sported a white Mohawk that flowed back into a long ponytail. For a moment, Xander imagined these last two looked at him and then back at the table where Buffy, Willow and Oz sat, before exchanging looks with each other.

Welcoming applause filled the Bronze. Xander made up for the lackluster response in the back of the room. "Come on, Vyxn!"

The lead singer slowly raised her microphone to her lips. She whispered, "We're so glad you came." She lowered her head demurely, then looked up at them through a loose fall of her hair and a glint in her eye. "This could be the last night of our lives."

A heartbeat. Then the drummer began a pounding rhythm, with the bass slipping in and out and the lead guitar wailing along with the mournful voice of the lead singer.

"This could be the last night of our lives,
Is the sky all red?
All the people dead?
And you can't believe a single word that she said
Was it all untrue?
Did she tell you lies?
In the final days . . . I'll be there for you."

Xander bobbed his head in time to the music.

At the table, Buffy looked away from the band and said to Willow and Oz, "Millennial stress syndrome?"

"She's off-key half the time," Oz noted, "but somehow it works."

"Maybe it's that leather harness she's wearing," Buffy said.

"No," Oz said. "It's her voice. It's very . . . distinctive."

"Distinctive in a Celine Dion kind of way?" Willow asked.

"But without the chest thumping," Buffy observed.

"And for good reason," Willow said. "I mean, with the skimpy harness and all."

The song ended to a long round of applause. The lead singer bowed her head slightly in acknowledgment. "Thank you, Sunnydale." She walked to the back of the stage and introduced the band members. The audience clapped after each name. "This is Nash on drums." Nash twirled a drumstick overhead, then struck it against a cymbal. "Carnie on bass. Playing lead guitar, Rave. And

I'm Lupa. Together we're Vyxn." She walked to the front of the stage again, an exaggerated sway to her hips, helped no doubt by the three-inch heels on her leather boots. "And we're just devastated."

Taking the cue, the white Mohawked lead guitarist began to play a medium-tempo chord. Black-haired Lupa began to sing forcefully.

> *"I'm devastated by you every day.*
> *My friends keep telling me to run away.*
> *But it's so hard for me,*
> *You're always killing me—with words. . . ."*

Xander couldn't help but notice as Cordelia entered the Bronze and intentionally crossed his line of sight. She made a point of ignoring him and veering away from the table where Buffy sat with Willow and Oz. She was determined to rejoin her lofty social circles but not above letting him know it was *his* loss. They were no longer a couple and she probably wanted to be as over him as he was over her. *Definitely over her,* Xander told himself. *Definitely.* Besides, thinking about the past was ruining his enjoyment of the music. He turned his undivided attention back to the stage.

After the second song, Xander jumped up and gave Vyxn a standing ovation. Buffy looked at him as if he had just sprouted antennae. *Actually,* she thought, *horns were probably a better analogy.* She looked around the Bronze and saw several other guys on their feet, clapping enthusiastically. Only guys. "Why am I not surprised?" she asked Willow.

Lupa turned her back to the audience and spread her arms to acknowledge her band. She looked to Carnie and Rave and said something not meant for the audience's ears. They both gave her a slight nod.

"Great, huh?" Xander said to Buffy and the gang sitting at the table behind him. But he had trouble taking his eyes off the band.

"They're not that good," Willow said, with a loyal look to Oz.

"They're okay," Oz, the Dingoes guitarist, admitted.

Lupa turned to the audience. "Thank you," she said. Xander gave a loud whoop. "Looks like we've got a big fan here already in Sunnydale," Lupa continued. She stepped down from the stage and walked over to Xander, trailing her microphone cord.

The closer she came, the deeper the frown on Buffy's face. Xander seemed totally enthralled in her presence. *Maybe he's just enthralled by the presence of so much cleavage,* she thought, dismissing her concern as unfounded. With a sigh, Buffy turned her attention to one of her textbooks, flipping aimlessly through the pages.

Lupa leaned her head down beside Xander's and whispered in his ear, "Tell me your name."

"Uh—uh—Xander," he said, beaming.

"Xander," she whispered, as if tasting the sound. The seductive way she pronounced it caused Xander to shiver visibly. Lupa felt as if she had just slipped a leash around his neck. There was special power in the knowing of names. She returned to the stage and said, "I'd like to dedicate this next song to our biggest Sunnydale fan, Xander. It's called 'Heartbreaker.' "

Xander turned to the table again. "She's dedicating a song to me!"

"Yeah," Buffy said. "We got that."

A driving drumbeat filled the Bronze. Lupa began to clap, a little awkwardly with the microphone held in one hand. Soon most in attendance were clapping in time to the song.

Alone at her table and excluding herself from the audience participation portion of the show, Cordelia swirled a straw around the half empty glass of soda. She almost jumped off her chair when someone tapped her on her shoulder.

"Cordelia?" he asked. "Cordelia Chase?" She turned. "You remember me, don't you?"

He was gorgeous. Tall, tan, with wind-swept blond hair, deep blue eyes and a dazzling smile. Even if she hadn't seen that smile on several television commercials and on the daytime soap "Wanderlust," she would have recognized him. They had dated for a couple months before he moved to Los Angeles two years ago.

"Of course I remember you," she said. She glanced briefly toward the stage but Xander remained ever clueless. "*Troy Douglas*. So great to see you again!"

CHAPTER 3

"Troy, I can't believe you're back in little old Sunnydale," Cordelia said over the swelling power ballad the Vyxn tramp had called "Heartbreaker."

"Visiting my mother for a couple weeks," he said. "But I was hoping we could catch up. Thought I might find you here."

"Not a lot of entertainment venues around here," Cordelia reminded him.

"Your friend seems to be enjoying himself," Troy said, nodding toward Xander, who was bobbing his head and slapping his knee.

"Who—him? He's not—I mean we're not friends—"

"You kept glancing over there," Troy explained. "I thought—"

"He's hard to miss, making a spectacle of himself over

there," Cordelia said. "Just no accounting for tasteless-ness."

Troy looked to Vyxn, listened for a few moments and decided, "They're not that bad."

"They're not that *good.*"

"I don't know. They kind of grow on you."

"Like a fungus."

Troy laughed. "Same old Cordelia."

"Well, you're looking good," she said. "No change there." He was smartly dressed in a chocolate brown jacket and a cream-colored, mock turtleneck.

"You still look great, Cordelia. I've really missed you."

"Thanks," she said. "But I read the tabloids. What about all those starlets throwing themselves at you?"

Troy grinned. "They pale in comparison."

"Still the sweet-talker," Cordelia said, but soaked up the compliment anyway.

"Maybe we could get a table in the back," Troy suggested. "Might be a little quieter. The music is a little . . . distracting."

"No argument here." Cordelia stood, grabbed her glass in one hand and placed her other hand on Troy's arm, entertaining the faint hope that Xander might glance and see that Cordelia Chase could do much better than date the likes of him. "Mind if we take a slight detour?"

"Not at all."

Cordelia led him to where Xander sat bopping to the music and stopped. "I thought you weren't—"

"We're not," Cordelia interrupted him.

Xander finally glanced up. "Cordelia? What's up?"

"Xander, do you remember Troy Douglas?" She paused for effect. "Before he became a big movie star and moved to L.A., he and I used to date. Each other."

Xander pointed at Troy. "Hey! I know you!" he said. "You're that SkinSure Pimple Boy!"

"That was a few years ago," Troy said.

"I never forget a pimply face."

"We're going to get a table in back," Cordelia said.

"Well, good. Good for you," Xander replied, a forced grin on his face.

Cordelia smiled, turned on her heel and walked off with her new guy in tow. Xander followed her progress for a moment but then the music pulled him back.

Xander sat through one song after another, barely giving Cordelia a second thought. Finally, the band finished their first set and Lupa announced they would take a ten-minute break. She ran her hands through her wild black hair and blew Xander a kiss, but as she walked offstage, her gaze drifted over to Buffy's table and her brow furrowed slightly.

Xander sighed and shook his head. He felt dazed, as if he'd been sleeping with his eyes open. When he glanced up, Buffy, Willow and Oz were standing beside him. Buffy and Willow were clutching their textbooks.

"Hey, Xander," Willow said. "Who's the guy with Cordelia? He seemed familiar."

"He's a real honey," Buffy commented, glancing back to where Xander assumed Cordelia and Troy were sitting.

"One of Cordelia's old flames," Xander said absently.

"Not really narrowing it down," Willow pointed out.

"Troy somebody," Xander said. "The SkinSure Pimple Boy."

"Oh, I know," Willow said. "Troy Douglas. He's that hot guy on *Wanderlust,* the soap opera." She cleared her throat. "Not that I actually watch those shows. But didn't he move to Los Angeles?"

"He's just visiting," Xander said.

"And yet Cordy is already making with the moves on him," Buffy noted.

"She's showing off," Xander said. "Just trying to make me jealous, I guess."

"Is it working?" Oz asked.

"No," Xander said. "Okay. A little bit. But I'm completely over her. I wonder if he has a limo? Cordelia is really impressed with limos."

"I'll leave it to you to find out," Buffy said. "We're leaving. I'm supposed to patrol with Angel and after that, a late night cuddled up with my red zone books."

"And I have that whole Sunnydale Hellmouth history to commit to paper," Willow said gloomily.

"Or not commit to paper," Oz suggested.

"That is the question," Willow said and groaned.

Xander craned his neck, looking for Cordelia. "I'll catch you guys later."

"Are you sure one of them is the Slayer?" Lupa asked Rave.

"I saw them dust a vampire," Rave said, smoothing her Mohawk-ponytail. "The redhead had a crossbow. The blonde had a stake."

"Only one can be the Slayer," Carnie said.

"But which one?" Lupa asked.

"Don't Slayers work alone?" Nash asked, fingering her spiked collar. "You said the Slayer worked alone. Four against one. Easy pickings, you said."

Lupa looked at herself in the mirror, which was bordered with small globe lights, half of them burnt out. "It's nothing we can't handle," Lupa said. She ran a heavily lacquered fingernail down her blushed cheek. In the wake of the nail's pressure, her skin shaded a mottled, reptilian green. In a moment her cheek was flushed human pink again. She had put their small troupe at risk, coming to this place, the Slayer's home turf. Yet while there was much at risk there was much to be gained. "Just a slight complication."

"Me, I don't like complications," Nash said. "Maybe it was a mistake coming here."

"Are you questioning my judgment?" Lupa asked, staring hard at Nash.

The drummer tugged at her collar for a moment before looking away. "Who me? I do what I'm told."

"See that you do." Lupa had always had the strongest voice for compulsion, even when their troupe had numbered a dozen, which meant she was not only the lead singer but the troupe leader as well. As troupe leader, her responsibilities were twofold: keep the troupe well fed and keep their numbers strong. The former had never been a problem. Once the pretty young boys heard her sing they would always come back for more. They just couldn't help themselves. And each successive night made the impulse that much stronger. And once she had the house full, had their complete and undivided attention, all Lupa had to do was look past the glare of the stage lights and decide which one of them would be the evening morsel. Personal contact, a few whispered suggestions and dinner practically served itself. No, the singing and the compulsion it engendered had never been a problem. Where Lupa had failed was in maintaining the strength of the troupe. In the past twenty-five years, since the day they had abandoned their distant home, their numbers had dwindled through disease, desertion and the occasional mishap. The last one to fall, Viola, had died at Lupa's own hands after she attempted to wrest leadership of the troupe from Lupa and disband Vyxn. Unwilling to let go of the old ways, Viola had always railed against the idea of performing in public. Her treachery had not been unexpected. *Well, Viola was old meat now. Let her rot.*

"Lupa?" Rave said. "You about ready?"

Lupa nodded, but couldn't resist reestablishing her authority before they went back on stage. "We will have our fill here as elsewhere. Did you see how easily I put the boy under my . . . influence?"

Carnie laughed. "That one's ripe for the plucking."

"He's one of them," Rave said. "He was with the Slayer, whichever one she is."

Lupa smiled. "You see," she said, looking specifically at Nash. "One less complication." She turned back to the mirror, adjusted her leather costume and briefly puckered her human lips—yet another layer of costuming. They walked as unseen predators, drifting among their helpless prey. Part of leadership, Lupa realized, was confidence, and she had much to be confident about. She retained firm control of the troupe with her goal close at hand. She sensed their fortunes were at a turning point. "And in the end, I *will* have the Slayer."

Xander decided to show Cordelia that her little display had had no effect on him whatsoever, so he casually made his way to her table. Only to find her laughing at something Troy had just said, staring into his eyes and touching his hand. All bad signs. Xander realized Cordelia was no longer playacting to make him jealous. So naturally, he was becoming jealous.

"Hey, Cordy," Xander called.

Cordelia gave him a withering stare. "Oh, is the teeny-bopper show over?"

"I see Acne Avenger has been making time while I've been enjoying the show."

"Look—Andrew, wasn't it?"

"Xander," Cordelia corrected Troy.

"Cordelia and I were just discussing old times."

"Besides," Cordelia said, "who I spend time with is none of your concern anymore."

"Right," Xander said, hardly mollified.

Cordelia smiled, not above fanning the flames a bit. "Xander, Troy was just telling me he's been nominated for a daytime Emmy."

"Daytime? Does that mean it has a curfew?"

"It's an award for soap opera acting," Cordelia said.

"Soap opera acting? There's an oxymoron for you." Xander said. "Like jumbo shrimp. Military intelligence."

Troy stood and pushed his chair back. Xander stood his ground.

Cordelia held her arms up between them. "Okay, maybe Xander doesn't realize many big stars got their start in soaps."

"Maybe," Troy said, sitting back down again.

"Xander?" Cordelia asked, squeezing his hand, which had, he just realized, curled into a fist.

"If you say so," Xander said.

"Excellent," Cordelia said. "Truce."

Just then, the crowd burst into applause, the male contingent more strenuously than the female. Xander looked over his shoulder and saw that Vyxn was taking the stage for their second set. His breath caught in his throat and he started to wonder how he had drifted so far from his stage-side seat. Demanding a response, Cordelia squeezed his hand again, hard.

"Y—yes?" he said.

"Troy and I were just about to step out for some fresh air," Cordelia was baring a dangerous smile. Xander realized that much.

"I—uh," Xander began. What he wanted to say, was about to say, was, *I'll join you after a couple of songs*. His gaze went from Cordelia to Troy and back again and felt the jealous sting anew. Just because he was over her didn't mean he couldn't play the part of a third wheel.

His forced smile was almost a grimace. "Fresh air? Love some."

They walked between the tables and past the stage toward the door. Xander looked back at the band and for a moment he thought that Lupa, the lead singer, winked directly at him. Maybe he just imagined it.

Rave drifted over to Lupa while she tuned her guitar. "Looks like you lost him," she whispered.

Lupa shook her head. "The hook is firmly set. Just a little play in the line for now. He'll be back. He won't be able to help himself. Plenty of time to reel him in."

"I just don't get it," Buffy said to Angel, as they walked down the street to her house. For once, they had had a quiet night of patrolling. Maybe Skull John's ranks were finally getting a little thin. With no vamps, demons or devil dogs in sight, Buffy even had time to crack open a book or two on top of a tombstone. Studying with Angel in the vicinity, however, was never all that productive. Well, not as long as you defined productive as actual retention of any textbook knowledge.

"But all the guys did?"

"Oh, the guys got it, all right," Buffy said. "Musically, Vyxn was just okay. Tolerable but uninventive."

"Well, you said it yourself," Angel said, quirking a smile.

"Right," Buffy said. "Extreme eye-candy factor."

"A girl band designed for guys."

"I suppose it's natural," Buffy said. "Of course, if it

was some buff guy band up there wearing leather Speedos with oiled pecs, I would hope I'd have enough composure not to drool all over my shoes."

"Of course not," Angel said. "Being ladylike—"

"Yes," Buffy said with a definitive nod.

"—you'd dab your chin with a napkin."

"I'd— Hey!" Buffy said and took a good-natured swipe at his smirking face. He leaned back and caught her arm, used it to pull her into an embrace. She fell into his arms willingly, tilted her head back, kissed his cool lips, and tried not to think about tomorrow. They only had a series of todays, all perfect moments in time with no thoughts of the future.

"I think this is where I get off," Buffy said. They had stopped walking in front of her house.

"See you tomorrow," he said.

For a moment, she thought she might cry. But she smiled bravely and backed up to her door, blew him a kiss, then unfastened the lock. When she turned back, he was gone and she wondered which of them the good-byes were hardest on.

As she drifted off to sleep, a math book open on her bed, she realized she was wrong. They had more than today. They had a history. And with that history, memories of an intimacy they could never share again. Since she couldn't make plans for the future and living in the past was too painful, Buffy simply dreamed of today. Her sleep was peaceful.

Not too far away, as Xander drifted off to sleep, content with the memory of having sabotaged Cordelia's

plans for a romantic evening with Troy just by hanging
out with them, a song drifted up from his subconscious,
through some mental back door, a musical virus on an
aural loop. In his semi-conscious state, he wasn't even
aware that he was humming the melody and murmuring
the lyrics into his pillow. *"In the final days . . . I'll be
there for you."*

CHAPTER 4

Solitaire soon discovered that Sunnydale, sitting atop the Hellmouth, had its own sewers and an extensive system of utility tunnels. So he was unsurprised to learn that a powerful vampire had decided to set up shop in Sunnydale in those very tunnels. Although more powerful than most humans, vampires were, to his way of thinking, weak-minded creatures. And what better place for an alpha male of the lot to cull a few cronies from the supernatural underworld than a place that drew them as flies to excrement.

Solitaire had one such weak-minded crony by the throat, dragging him through a dimly lit tunnel. This particular vampire called himself Marcus. He had decided to cooperate wholeheartedly with Solitaire's desire to find his fearless leader shortly after Solitaire removed one of the vampire's hands with a meat cleaver. Marcus seemed rather upset at his loss. "Now it will just be like hunting humans with one hand tied behind your back," Solitaire had told him. Marcus cradled the stump against his chest and whimpered about how Skull John would show Solitaire who ran the show in Sunnydale. He hadn't even been able to maintain a properly menacing vampface after the amputation. *Don't make vampires like they used to,* Solitaire thought.

They came to a T intersection. "Stop whining," Solitaire said, "or I'll rip your other hand off and stuff it down your throat. Which way?"

Marcus nodded to the right, as if voicing the direction would be a greater betrayal to Skull John than a simple bob of the head.

Solitaire twisted the vampire's good arm behind his back and pushed him forward. "How close?"

"Close," Marcus said. "You'll regret this."

"Shut up," Solitaire said without revealing any nervousness. Skull John would present a much more difficult challenge than had Warhammer. *A mistake will be more costly this time. Probably fatal.* Yet this battle would take his true measure, would show him if he was ready to take on the Slayer he had heard about.

Just ahead, the tunnel opened into a large cavern with multiple points of egress. Against the far wall was a chair draped in black velvet. Slouched on the ersatz throne was the largest vampire Solitaire had ever come across. He was bare-chested and did indeed look formidable, even more so for the dozen human skulls he wore strung as a necklace around his neck.

His throne room was less impressive. An unframed

print of Hieronymus Bosch's *Hell* adorned one rough wall, held in place by masking tape. To the right, against the wall, was a long wooden table fitted with leather straps placed at five points, to secure head, wrists and ankles of human captives. Bloodstains, some black, some still sticky fresh, covered the tabletop. Rickety, ladder-back chairs ringed the table. Orange plastic milk crates, no doubt stolen from a convenience store, lined the left wall of the chamber. A couple of oil-burning lanterns hung from wall hooks provided meager illumination.

For all his posturing, Skull John looked like the type of imposing vampire who had grown tired of the hunt and simply waited for his underlings to bring him his meals. Solitaire could even imagine Skull John draining the veins and arteries of his victims into a large goblet before drinking the still-warm blood. The goblet would be, he thought, gold-plated.

Skull John sat up straighter and glared at his visitor and his captive. "What is this? Who are you?" he demanded.

"Marcus here tells me you're in charge of this little fiefdom," Solitaire said.

"Apparently Marcus has a big mouth," Skull John said. "Be sure, he will suffer a penalty."

"Don't bother," Solitaire said, reaching into one pocket of his flowing black overcoat. "This one's on me." Solitaire withdrew a smoothly milled wooden stake. Marcus's big mouth opened a little farther, this time in astonishment. His face transformed into its convoluted vampiric countenance as his fangs appeared. He struggled, hissing in fear, but Solitaire had him firmly under control as he slammed the wooden stake into his chest. Solitaire snapped the necklace with its little metal skull free of Marcus's neck an instant before the one-handed vampire vanished in an explosion of dust. Solitaire brushed errant dust from his hands and his red leather vest, then he tossed the necklace at Skull John's feet. "You'll want to find a replacement for this. But first, I have a few questions."

"I would have made him suffer more," Skull John said, stepping down from his velvet-covered chair. He stood with his fists on his hips, classically defiant, still in control of the situation. "Now, who the hell are you? And excluding, for the moment, random insanity, what brings you to my lair?"

"Most call me Solitaire."

Skull John scratched his chin, a movement that set the human skulls on his necklace clattering together like macabre wind chimes. "Solitaire. . . ." he said, then his eyes widened. "Ah—I've heard that name! More than a century ago. You're the one they talk about, the vampire who walks in the sun."

"Since my reputation precedes me," Solitaire remarked, "I presume you will comply with my request for information."

Skull John barked a laugh. "You think I should be afraid? Tell you everything you want to know? Listen, Solitaire, Day Walker or not, down here we're the same, you and I. I am your equal. Cancel that. Down here, I am your superior." He picked up Marcus's broken necklace. "Maybe *you* should be the one to wear this next. To demonstrate your fealty."

Solitaire grinned. "If you tell me what I want to know, you can maintain the delusion of your own superiority." *Goad him along,* Solitaire thought. *He'll never tell me what I want to know until I force it out of him.*

"All right, let's play your game," Skull John said. He walked back and forth in small arcs, as if sizing up the competition. Solitaire suspected that Skull John was hoping to lull him into a moment of inattention before he made his move. "What exactly do you think I know?"

"The name of the Slayer."

"There's a Slayer hereabouts?" Skull John asked innocently. "And no one thought to tell me."

"I know the Slayer is here," Solitaire said. "She would be drawn to this place. Just as you were. And I'm sure she's dusted a few of your cronies already."

"I come and go where I please. No concerns about this Slayer."

"Another delusion. Fine," Solitaire said. "Now tell me her name."

"If I did know her name, why would I tell you?"

"Because I'm going to do you a favor, Johnny," Solitaire said. "I'm going to kill her for you."

Skull John laughed. "Better vamps than you have tried."

"It's a win–win situation," Solitaire said. "You have nothing to lose."

"Go home and forget about the Slayer. She's out of your league." He snapped his fingers. From each of the two tunnels flanking the throne chair, a hulking vampire appeared. They were large, in full demonic vampface, fangs prominent. Both wore black T-shirts, the fealty necklaces and khaki pants. Solitaire realized they were twins. "Now get the hell out of here. Kyle and Carl will show you the way."

"Tell me," Solitaire goaded. "What *league* do you have to be in to have somebody else fight your battles?"

Skull John stepped forward and displayed his own vampface and fangs. He hissed, "I stopped taking out the garbage years ago."

Solitaire struck him with a right jab, flattening his nose. Skull John roared and charged him, arms wide. Letting Skull John's momentum carry them both down, Solitaire rolled on his back and thrust a foot out, hurling Skull John against the wall, where several of the skulls on his necklace shattered, dribbling canines and molars.

Before Skull John could shake off the impact, Solitaire was back on his feet and in two quick strides landed a solid kick in Skull John's stomach, lifting him off the ground. Skull John swatted one of Solitaire's legs out from under him and grabbed his head between his hands. He tried to remove Solitaire's head as if it were a twist-off bottle cap and never saw the uppercut that slammed his jaw shut so hard that one of his fangs shattered.

Skull John sidestepped and pulled an oil lantern off a hook and brought it down in both hands toward Solitaire's head. Solitaire raised a forearm in time to shatter the glass housing and swat the lantern aside. It crashed on top of the wooden table and he heard a whoosh of flames behind him. He ducked low, grabbed Skull John around the upper thighs and hurled him over his head right onto the burning table.

Roaring, Skull John tried to roll off the table, even as he swatted at the flames scorching his bare back and arms. Solitaire scooped up one of the rickety chairs and smashed it over Skull John's head as he fell from the table.

Staggering away from Solitaire and the burning table, Skull John yelled to his twin henchmen, "Don't just stand there!"

Immediately, Kyle—or was it Carl?—whipped the black velvet cloth off of Skull John's throne and tossed it over the flames to extinguish them.

"Not the fire, you fool," Skull John shouted as he stumbled back to the wall.

Carl sidestepped his brother and made a move toward Solitaire, but he was too late. Solitaire grappled with the stunned vampire leader and had him in a death grip before Carl had taken three steps. Carl froze.

"Don't just stand there!" Skull John shouted. "Waste him!"

Now both brothers crept forward.

Solitaire had a stake against Skull John's chest before they could get their hands on him. "One more step and I dust him. Two more steps and I dust the both of you after." He looked at Skull John's grimacing face. "Call them off."

"Do as he says," Skull John whispered, just loud enough for them to hear and obey.

The vampire twins stopped, seemingly happy with the turn of events. Solitaire thought they were cautiously optimistic that they would live to bite another day. Solitaire tightened his grip just enough to assure Skull John's full attention. "Her name?"

"Summers," Skull John replied. "Buffy Summers."

"Good boy, Johnny," Solitaire said. "Anything else I should know?"

Skull John looked confused, apprehensive. "What? No, nothing."

"I'm going to let you live," Solitaire said. "You know why? No, don't answer. I'll tell you why. I need you and your goons to stay out of the picture until I've had my little dance with the Slayer. Not that I think any one of your crew is a match for her one on one, but your type probably likes to hunt in gangs. So, forget about it. Leave her to me."

"Leave her to you," Skull John repeated, but not convincingly.

"See, now I've changed my mind," Solitaire said. "I guess I will kill you after all." He pulled the stake back just enough to give the thrust some force.

"Wait! Wait! There is something else."

"Much better," Solitaire said, but kept the stake poised in striking position. "Let's hear it."

"There's a rumor that she . . . she has a pet vampire," Skull John said, "who watches her back."

"A pet vampire, hmm?" Solitaire wondered why a vampire would aid a Slayer. *In exchange for his life, perhaps. Even so, why would a Slayer suffer a vampire to live. Curious.* "An interesting tidbit."

"Thought you'd like that," Skull John said, confident again.

"Yes, very good," Solitaire said. More for the benefit of the twins, who could see him, than for Skull John, who could not, Solitaire flashed a set of impressive fangs and an equally pronounced vampiric face. "Bye-bye."

"What—?" The stake was in Skull John's heart that fast. Another explosion of dust followed. Then the strand of skulls clattered to the floor.

"You killed him," Kyle said, staring dumbfounded at the skulls on the ground, the only evidence that his vampire lord had been standing there a moment ago.

"He was annoying," Solitaire said.

Carl cleared his throat. All the time he needed to change his allegiance. "I always thought so."

"Johnny had a bad attitude," Solitaire said. "You boys, on the other hand, do what you're told. Right?" They both nodded quickly. "So, spread the word to the rest of Skull John's goons. From now on, they and you listen to me and only me. For now, I'll keep it simple. Keep your hands off the Slayer. I doubt that will be too much of a hardship for you. Understood?" More nods. "Any questions?" Shaking heads. "Good," he said, smiling. "Gentlemen, I think we've reached consensus."

They almost smiled in relief.

"And one more thing," Solitaire added. "Lose those stupid necklaces."

After Solitaire had gone, the vampire twins noticed that he'd left a playing card—a queen of diamonds—on the floor, lying within the necklace of skulls.

As Xander made his way to his locker after lunch, he stopped short at the sudden realization that he couldn't recall the content of any of his morning classes. While his body had been slouched in his usual seat in each classroom, his mind had wandered back to the previous night's Vyxn performance. *Sometimes you just can't get a song out of your head.* No big deal, he figured. Vyxn would be long gone in a few days and things would return to what passed for normal at Hellmouth central. *Might as well enjoy the diversion while I can.*

He glimpsed Oz at his locker, fishing a textbook out from the bottom of a pile. So Xander veered across the hallway, stopping to rap his knuckles on the open locker door. "Hey, Oz."

"Hey."

"See you at the show tonight?"

"Wouldn't miss it," Oz said, swinging the door shut with a clang.

Between classes, Buffy waited near the checkout counter of the library while Giles tried to pull his attention out of one of his particularly oversized volumes, a Who's Who in the Demon Underworld, she was sure. "Anybody home?" she asked finally.

"I'm sorry, Buffy," Giles said, with one last look at the passage he'd been reading. "Quiet patrol last night, you say?"

"Not a creature was stirring," she replied. "I even managed to log some quality study time."

"Really?"

"You don't have to look so surprised, Giles," Buffy declared. "I do read the occasional textbook lesson. Sometimes more than once."

"No, no, Buffy, I just meant that it's gratifying to see you've been able to achieve some balance in your life."

"Good thing, too," Buffy replied. "I got corralled into

a morning pep talk with my new guidance counselor. She believes one can never study enough."

"I would tend to agree with her—except, of course, in the case of the Slayer."

"Of course," Buffy said sweetly. "So, any progress on the identity of our flesh-eater? Since I haven't seen any revivified corpses staggering around Weatherly Park, I vote we rule out zombies."

"Agreed," Giles said. "Willow has turned up some missing persons reports but we've found no references to human bones. So far, we have a solitary victim. Since all references to ghouls indicate they travel in packs, I would expect a great deal more carnage. Moreover, I found no specific references in the Watcher journals to ghouls preying in this country. However, there would appear to be any number of creatures with a taste for human flesh."

"Terrific," Buffy said. "We're demon delicacies."

"There is one in particular, a fascinating creature at least seven feet tall." Giles reached for the ancient tome he'd left on the counter and spun it around for her to get a better look at the crude, hand-drawn picture on the open page.

She read the caption. "The Rasselu demon."

Giles nodded and read her a short passage. "With its head and hands perpetually cast in magical flame, the Rasselu demon roasts its victims alive, then strips off and devours their fl—"

"Please," Buffy said, holding up a hand. "I just had the mystery meat for lunch. Could we read the rest later?"

Xander and Oz sat at a table close to the stage. They had both ordered sodas, but their glasses were down to melting ice cubes and they hadn't bothered to reorder. Even though Vyxn had not yet come onstage for their second night's performance, Xander was having trouble focusing on the conversation. He kept looking to the stage for some sign, any sign that the band was about to begin their show.

"So Will's not coming?" he asked Oz. He couldn't remember if he'd already asked that particular question.

"She's agonizing over this history paper," Oz said. "She sees it as a challenge to her integrity."

"You've offered to help?"

"Of course."

"And?"

"Integrity again," Oz said. "Says it's her decision. Gotta respect that."

"Maybe they should grade integrity on a curve," Xander said. *I wonder if Vyxn will be wearing the same costumes.* "Then you would get points for good intentions."

"Good intentions?" Oz asked wryly.

Xander nodded. "Yeah, since they're not just for paving the road to hell, anymore."

Oz had decided to give Willow some space, yet he still found it odd that he was sitting in the Bronze, hanging out with Xander. *As good a place as any,* he thought. But it was more than that. He had been thinking about the lead singer's distinctive voice through most of the day. Coming to the Bronze seemed a good way, the perfect way, to prove to himself that it had been nothing more than his imagination adding some element of mystery, of enchantment that wasn't really there.

The crowd cheered as the band took the stage. Oz

hardly noticed that most of the patrons were male tonight. He didn't care that the band performed the same songs in the same order with the same amount of theatrics as they had their first night. Lupa's voice really *was* distinctive.

Oz realized he'd been staring at the band for quite a while when somebody crossed his line of sight. He looked up and saw Cordelia, Troy beside her. "Hello, Xander," Cordelia said, standing practically in front of him.

"Oh, hi, Cordy," he said, craning his neck a little to see the stage behind her.

"Figured you couldn't get enough of the trashy bondage babes."

"Further evidence of my bad taste," Xander replied. "You'll recall I used to date you."

"Enjoy the show, Xander. Someday maybe you'll actually get a life." She led Troy to an empty table.

Xander didn't bother to track her progress. "She's gone, right?" he asked Oz without looking away from the stage.

"Definitely," Oz said and found himself staring as well . . . until Willow stepped in front of him. Oz glanced around and saw Angel and Buffy standing beside her. Buffy was eyeing Angel curiously as he checked out the band.

"Hey, babe," Oz said to Willow, staying focused on her with some effort.

"Hey," Willow said, and then deflated a bit when she saw that his full attention was not forthcoming. She turned to Angel, as if to explain Oz's faux pas. "She has a very distinctive voice."

"Angel, you're a guy," Buffy said to him. "Cast your

vote? Major label, independent label, wedding and bar mitzvah gigs or perpetual garage band?"

"I might be slightly outside their target age demographic."

"Noted," Buffy said. "Now pull the lever."

"Aside from their obvious physical charms . . ." Angel began.

"No need to linger there."

"Musically?" Angel asked.

Buffy nodded.

"They're . . . competent."

"Competent?"

Angel nodded. "There's no flourish, no passion in their playing. It's hard to explain. Maybe it's just that they don't seem to . . . have experienced what their songs are about."

"See," Buffy said to Willow. "No reason to go gaga."

Willow surveyed the crowd, her gaze finally settling on Oz before she looked to Buffy. "And yet, there's a whole lot of gaga going on." Willow pulled up a chair and sat partially in front of Oz. He noticed her and raised his eyebrows. "Oz, want to help me look for something?"

"Now?"

"Now would be good."

"O . . . okay," Oz said. "I'm good."

She took his hand and looked at Buffy. "I have an idea I'd like to check. It might be nothing."

"Okay, Will," Buffy said. "Be careful. Angel and I will probably do a patrol through Weatherly Park before I settle down for some good old-fashioned fun with schoolbooks." Oz and Willow left, holding hands, but Oz kept looking back over his shoulder at the stage. The lead singer of Vyxn was whispering in some guy's ear.

Angel was watching the band with the intense look he usually reserved for her. "Hey," Buffy said, nudging him. "You're not going gaga after all, are you?"

He immediately looked down at her. "No," he said. "It's just that her voice . . . There's just something . . ."

"Distinctive?" Buffy asked, frowning.

"Different," Angel said.

CHAPTER 5

For some reason Sunnydale Cemetery always seemed darker than its surroundings. This night a steady breeze rustled leaves and stirred scraps of paper around, creating enough ambient noise to keep the pair constantly throwing glances to this side or that. They were all too aware that there were real things out there to go bump in the night. Sometimes a little knowledge is a frightening thing. "Are you sure this is a good idea?" Oz asked as he led Willow back to the bush in Sunnydale Cemetery where he originally found the leg bone.

"No," Willow admitted.

"And yet, here we are."

"But I've come prepared. See?" Willow said and handed Oz one of two wooden stakes she'd brought for the occasion. "I took them from the stash in the library."

"One Slayer and we're all set," Oz said wryly.

"We've done some amateur slaying on our own, now and then."

"This is true."

"Besides, this shouldn't take long," Willow said. She crouched down and looked around the bush.

"What?"

"Confirmation," Willow said, distracted. "Some form of identity that connects the leg bone."

"To the shin bone?"

"I came across a police report about a missing UC Sunnydale freshman," Willow explained. "Robert John Wallace. Reported missing two days ago. I thought maybe we'd find something to prove the leg bone belonged to him. Not that that would do Robert any good, but at least we could solve the mystery." After a few more minutes of searching the surrounding ground, gravestones and statuary, Willow stood up straight, stretched her back and sighed. "Nothing," she said, clearly disappointed.

"We did look before," Oz said, referring to the night he'd discovered the bone.

"We were looking for the rest of his—or her—bones," Willow said. "I was hoping, maybe, we overlooked something dark, like a wallet or something. Anything." She stood up. "Sorry I wasted your time."

"With Willow Rosenberg?" Oz wrapped an arm around her shoulders. "How could I possibly be wasting time?"

Willow smiled.

Something skittered along the pavement on the other side of the iron fence. Startled, they both looked past the fence for the source of the sound. Willow sighed as she saw the empty potato chip bag skip, skip, tumble down the sidewalk . . . right past the glint of light. "What's that?"

"What?"

She pointed. "Right near the base of that tree." It gleamed with reflected light from the street lamps. "Something metallic."

"Empty soda can?" Oz said.

"No," Willow said. "It's too small for that."

She ran back the way they had come. "Hey! Wait up!" Oz called, worried that, in her single-mindedness, she'd slam into a newly risen vampire looking for his first drink of forever.

He caught up to her as she reached the entrance to the cemetery. Together they jogged along the fence until they came to the tree opposite the bush where Oz had found the bone. "Where is it . . . ?" Willow said, looking around intently. "It's gone— No! Here!"

"What is it?"

She looked at him. "A ring," she said, turning it in her hands. "A class ring. Sunnydale High. With the razor-back logo and everything. Ooh, look!" She handed it to him.

"What am I—?"

She adjusted it to gather the light. "Inside!"

Oz tilted the thick, gold ring at a slightly different angle. He read the inscription. Just three initials: RJW.

Back at the Bronze, Cordelia was having a hard time keeping Troy focused on their conversation. With his elbow resting on the table and his chin perched on the heel of his palm, his gaze kept drifting from her face to the stage. At first she tried to ignore this lapse in manners, but after Xander had pretended to ignore her one too many times she was starting to get irritated with the entire male gender.

"So, Troy," she said, turning his face back toward her. "What's it really like, starring in a soap opera?"

"It's . . . um . . . a little . . . uh," he stammered. "This band kind of grows on you, doesn't it?"

"Like a fungus," she said. "Remember? You didn't answer my question."

"No . . . I . . . uh, acting in a soap opera, right?"

"Right."

He made a valiant attempt to stay focused on the conversation. "For an actor, it's a little frustrating because you don't have a lot of takes to get it right. Viewers see five hours of *Wanderlust* each week, but it takes eight to ten hours a day of filming to produce those five hours. Even spreading it around between all the actors, it's still a grueling pace."

Now it was Cordelia's turn to drift. Only she was looking at Xander, a few tables away, bobbing his head in rhythm to the music, oblivious to his surroundings. "Can you believe him?"

"What—who?"

"Xander Harris, that's who!" Cordelia said. She looked at Troy who, unfortunately, took that moment to return his attention to Lupa's mournful singing. Cordelia brushed his hand out from under his chin. "Is that all it takes for you guys to trance out? Women wearing strips of leather?"

"In all fairness, they are strategically placed strips of leather."

"I don't find this very amusing."

"Neither do I," Troy said.

"Then let's leave."

"Now?"

"Right this instant," Cordelia said. She grabbed her purse in one arm and Troy by the elbow with her free hand. She made a point of steering them past Xander's table on the way out. "Good-bye, Xander," Cordelia said. "I'm leaving. With Troy."

Xander blinked a couple times and looked up at her. "Cool," he said, a little distractedly. "Don't do anything I wouldn't do."

She smiled wickedly. "Believe me, that won't be a problem."

A moment after she had stormed off, with Troy willingly in tow, Xander looked toward the door in a moment of clarity. "What just happened?" he asked himself.

The next moment, Lupa launched into another song and his attention returned to the stage, his budding awareness vanishing before the second verse.

Buffy and Angel walked along a dirt path in Weatherly Park, her gaze returning again and again to the tree line or any row of bushes large enough to conceal a ravenous, card-carrying member of the Hellmouth Society. They came in all shapes and sizes, but most of them were big and ugly and all of them saw humans as prey. Some, as the vampires, wanted human blood. Others, as their current mystery predator or predators, ate of human flesh. The rest generally preferred to snack down on a human soul or two before calling it a night. Buffy could never decide which were the creepiest, but never agonized overly much on the fiendish rankings since her mission was pretty much the same regardless of their inhuman appetites: slay them.

Slung over her shoulder, in what was probably unwarranted optimism, was her backpack. She was more likely to need Mr. Pointy before she'd have the opportunity to crack a textbook. Fate had made her the Slayer and that role always threatened to take over her life. Yet the thought of having to repeat her senior year while Willow, Oz and Xander, not to mention Cordelia, moved on to bigger and better, or at least different, things was enough to give her more nightmares than the latest soul-sucking demon to enter town. She was determined to squeeze a little joy out of the normal things in life, even if they included the frightening world of college.

Joy also came in the time she spent alone with Angel, even though their relationship was anything but normal or ordinary, she being a seventeen-year-old high school student and he being a two-hundred-and-forty-odd-year-old vampire who just happened to have a soul and with it, a human conscience. That made all the difference. Sometimes, she could almost pretend that they were normal girlfriend slash boyfriend. Especially on such a cool, breezy night.

"So they do nothing special for you?" Buffy asked, for about the third time. Of course, she was talking about Vyxn. "No drooling obsession?"

"No," Angel said, smiling, "but I'm beginning to wonder about you."

"Who? Me?" Buffy said. "I'm just glad you aren't all caught up in them like . . ." Like what? Like normal guys? Was Angel's lack of a response to Vyxn just a reminder that he was not normal boyfriend material?

"Like who?"

"Nobody," Buffy said. "You're right. I'm obsessing. Next topic."

"Okay. You name it."

"Well," Buffy said, "we could talk about how I'm failing three courses and will probably have to repeat my senior year. Or we could talk about these flesh-eaters, which is probably a lot more pleasant subject." She spun around to face Angel and that's when she noticed it.

She stepped off the path.

"What is it?" Angel asked.

A row of hedges by the perimeter fence. All neatly trimmed. Basically identical. Except for one. "Look at these hedges," she said.

"What about them?"

"Not all of them," Buffy said. "This one."

One in the middle of the row was different, darker. It would have been a lot more obvious in daylight. At night, it was a subtle difference. The tiny leaves were brown and crumbled in her fingers. She broke off some of the twiglike ends. Angel stepped up beside her and frowned. "It's dead," he said.

"Or at least dying," Buffy said, crouching down at the base and finding that the dirt around it was loose. As she brushed aside some of the soil, her knuckles rubbed up against a hard surface. She brushed some more, revealing something pale. She rapped her knuckles against it and looked up at Angel. "Plywood?"

Angel squatted down beside her and together they worked their fingers under the edge of the plywood and lifted it up, revealing a pit. A skull stared back at her from the hole, a beetle scurrying into an empty eye socket. Startled, she lost her grip and fell back on her rear end with an *oomph!*

Angel dropped the plywood and looked at her, concerned. "What was it? What did you see?"

"Bones," Buffy said. "A lot of bones."

Angel turned back to the exposed plywood, hoisted it up, then shoved it aside to expose the mound of bones. Buffy brushed herself off and joined him. "That's not all that's down here," he said, reaching down through the bones for something dark and long.

At first, Buffy imagined it was a snake, but snakes rarely came with brass buckles. "A belt?"

Angel shifted several long bones aside and brought up something else. "A wallet," he said, flipping it open.

Buffy looked over his shoulder and said, "Credit card, automobile club card, UC Sunnydale ID. Tony Lima."

Angel looked at Buffy in that grim way he had since the first time she had met him three years ago. It was a look designed to make her worry, for her own good. It usually worked. "There's more," he said. "A lot more."

After watching almost an entire Vyxn show, Xander felt physically drained. Somehow, the four women in the band had seemed to become more energized as one number led into the next. He had always thought putting on a live concert would be exhausting for the band. Yet, Vyxn seemed to revel in the attention. *Some people are just born for show business,* he guessed.

When the band thanked everyone after their second encore, Xander was almost too weary to drag himself out of his cushioned seat and head home. He looked around. Most of the other guys looked as sluggish as he felt. Oddly, most of the female Bronze patrons had left. *Well, not all that odd,* he corrected. If they had come with dates, they were probably as annoyed with them as Cordelia had been with Xander and Troy. Right now, all he wanted to do was stagger home and plop his body down in bed and get some sleep.

Somebody tapped him on the shoulder.

Xander turned back toward the stage and stared at the one with the wild red hair. Carnie. He couldn't believe his good fortune. He attempted to sit up straighter and it was more of a feat than he would have imagined. Then he noticed another one, the one with the long white Mohawk haircut that flowed back into a ponytail. Her name escaped him for a moment and she seemed to realize it.

"I'm Rave," she said. She pointed to Carnie. "And this is Carnie."

"Listen, you gals are great," he said, almost stumbling over his words. "Cool band. And I'm not just saying that because you're—" He was about to say "because you're half naked."

"Because we're beautiful?" Carnie asked, grinning. She sat down on Xander's right, her bare thigh almost brushing his trouser leg.

"Right," Xander said. "That's, uh, exactly what I was gonna say. Beauty and, um, talent. Two great things that go well together."

"Lupa says you're a big fan," Rave said.

She pulled up a chair and sat on his left. Lots more exposed leg for him to ogle, but he tried to maintain eye contact. "The biggest," Xander said.

"That's why she dedicated 'Heartbreaker' to you last night."

"That was really . . . really great," Xander said. *I'm so lame,* he thought.

"Would you like," Carnie said, pausing to wink, "an autograph?"

"Uh—yes, that's sure what I would like," Xander said, mentally kicking himself as he slid a damp cocktail napkin across his small table. Both Rave and Carnie signed their names with a flourish. No last names. "Thanks," Xander said. "Big time."

"You know," Rave said, scratching her chin with an ornately lacquered fingernail. In the shadow, Xander thought the scratched skin turned a darker shade, but not red. A trick of the light, he decided. "We were wondering about something."

"Oh?" Xander said, several wild fantasies beginning to take form.

"About those girls at your table," Carnie said.

"Oh, that, um, you mean Cordelia? The one dragging Fashion Boy around like a puppy dog?"

Carnie threw an odd look at Rave and said, "The blonde and the one with hair like mine." She fingered her wild red locks and Xander belatedly realized she meant Willow. But Carnie's hair was unnaturally red, cherry red, straight from a bottle filled with all man-made ingredients whereas Willow came by her color naturally. "That would be Buffy and Willow. Willow's the one with, um, red hair."

"Buffy and Willow . . ." Rave said, as if testing the names. "We thought they looked familiar. We thought maybe we had met them before."

Carnie stood. "No, those names aren't familiar."

Rave also stood, backing away from Xander. "It must have been the light, that's all."

"Well," Xander said, getting to his feet and tripping over a table leg. "Sorry I couldn't be more help to you ladies, but, uh, thanks for the autographs. Guess . . . guess I'll see you some more tomorrow."

Carnie smiled broadly and blew him a kiss. "I'm sure you will."

Xander backed awkwardly away from them, bumped into a table and spun around, hurrying toward the exit, not sure what had just happened.

As he bumbled out the door, an odd thought occurred to him about Carnie and Rave. Their complexions had been flawless. Nevertheless, that wasn't the strange part. They'd been playing energetically under hot stage lights for several hours and somehow—after all that exertion—they hadn't perspired at all.

Rave looked at Carnie, raised an eyebrow. "So?"

Carnie shrugged. "Now we know their names."

"Lupa's not going to be happy with just their names."

Carnie waved a hand dismissively. "We can't just come right out and ask him which one's the Slayer."

"He'd probably spill his guts for Lupa," Rave said, then laughed at the image she'd conjured inadvertently.

"Then let Lupa ask the questions," Carnie said. "Besides, it's too soon and this place is too public. What if he became suspicious and bolted? Lupa brought us here. She can take the risks."

"You're right," Rave said. "Did you see them, though? They couldn't get enough. This is easier than the college crowd."

"Maybe we're just getting better at it," Carnie said. They both laughed.

CHAPTER 6

Joyce Summers placed a glass of orange juice in front of her daughter, cleared her throat and said, "Buffy, I had a call from a Mrs. Burzak at your school yesterday."

Buffy dropped her unbitten bran muffin back on the saucer. "The guidance counselor from *The Twilight Zone*.

"She's very concerned about your academic standing," Joyce said. "She talked about red—"

"Zones," Buffy finished. "Red zones, yellow zones. I know all about the zones."

"It's just her—"

"System," Buffy said. "I know."

"Well, Buffy, I hope you're taking this seriously," Joyce said. "You could jeopardize your chances to get into college."

"Right, Mom."

Joyce sat down, sipped her coffee and took a moment. "Buffy, I know that the—I mean your—"

"Slaying."

"Right," Joyce said and cleared her throat. "The slaying." Buffy knew that her mother still wasn't comfortable with the role fate had chosen for her daughter. At first, her mother had assumed being the Slayer was something Buffy had chosen for herself, like a macabre hobby. But it was more than that and they both knew it. Buffy's role as Slayer would end only when her life ended. Her mother knew that now, at least intellectually. Still, she wanted her daughter to have and experience all the normal things a teenage girl should, including boyfriends, college, career and, eventually, a family of her own.

Joyce started over again. "I know that slaying is a part of your life, a part of who you are," she said. "But you are so much more than that. You have such incredible . . . potential."

"My mother," Buffy said. "My cheerleader."

"I just want you to remember that there's more to life, to *your* life, than—"

"—than killing big, ugly, nasty things?"

"Right," Joyce said with a quick grin.

"I know, Mom," Buffy said. "Believe me, I'm worried about these . . . red zone things, too. I really do want to go to college, Mom."

Giles turned the high school class ring over in his hand until the initials were visible. "RJW," Giles said. "I suppose we can rule out coincidence, given the circumstances. Good work, Willow."

Willow beamed. "Thank you, Giles. Oz helped, too."

"She's being modest," Oz said. "Willow of the eagle eye."

"Just the same," Giles said. "I'm relieved Willow didn't attempt to find this on her own. Willow, how is your paper on the history of Sunnydale progressing?"

"If I leave out the high mortality rates, missing persons and strange occurrences of, well, it's—I have lots of three-by-five index cards. That has to be a good, right?"

Oz nodded supportively.

Giles frowned. "Very good. I'm sure you'll do what's best."

The library door swung open as Buffy entered, carrying textbooks in one arm and supporting a duffel bag over her shoulder with the other. Giles smiled, straightened up and realized that he had unconsciously hidden the ring in his fist when he'd heard the door. "Buffy," Giles called. "Good, you're here. Willow has identified the victim by matching a missing persons report to a high school class ring she and Oz found just outside the cemetery."

"Great," Buffy said. "But we're not done yet."

"What do you—?" Giles started to ask just as Buffy lifted the old duffel bag onto the checkout counter.

She told them about her previous night's patrol with Angel in Weatherly Park. "We found a pit filled with more bones, lots of bones . . . and this," she said and up-ended the duffel bag, dumping a pile of wallets, wristwatches, rings and other jewelry on the counter.

* * *

Joyce Summers was just leaving for the art gallery when the doorbell rang. She looked through the peephole and saw a tall, broad-shouldered man with a pale face. He had a pronounced widow's peak, though his pale blond hair had such a severe crew cut that she could plainly see his scalp. *Probably ex-military,* she thought. He wore a long black overcoat and a pair of wire-frame eyeglasses that reminded her of pictures of Teddy Roosevelt. He was carrying a large black case and appeared disarmingly distracted. She opened the door. "May I help you?"

"Quite possibly," the man said. The bright, sunny day caused him to squint his eyes. She imagined his skin was probably sensitive to the sun, judging from his complexion. "You came highly recommended by an associate."

"Is this about the gallery?" Joyce asked.

"Correct," he said. "The . . . art gallery."

"You're an art dealer?"

"A dealer in Sumerian antiquities. May I?" he said, indicating the door. "I have some samples I'd love to show you."

"Well, I was just about to head over to the gallery, but I suppose I have a minute," Joyce said. "Come in."

"Thank you ever so much," he said, with a nod and a grin. "I do hope I can make this worth your while." He stepped into the foyer and unfastened the button of his black overcoat. As the coat opened, Joyce caught a glimpse of his red leather vest.

"We know Robert John Wallace was reported missing only two days ago," Giles said. "Whatever devoured him was fast and certainly thorough."

"Now that Buffy and Angel have found a whole, um, hole filled with bones, we know he wasn't the first victim," Willow said.

"And the jewelry and wristwatches would seem to rule out theft as a contributing motive," Giles said.

Oz had been flipping through the wallets and other personal effects Buffy had brought to the library. Now he looked up. "Have you noticed all this stuff belonged to male victims?"

"Not one purse in the pit," Buffy added.

"Not just the wallets," Oz said. "These large watch faces. Men's watches."

Giles took a closer look, nodded. "Oz is correct. The class rings are exclusively men's rings. The other rings and necklaces all have a masculine design to them."

Xander entered the library, looking a little sleepy-eyed. He spotted the pile of personal effects and started flipping through the items. "Somebody raid the lost and found? I had a pair of galoshes in third grade if anyone—"

"Xander," Willow said. "Buffy and Angel found these things in a pit of human bones."

Xander quickly dropped the thick, gold-plated bracelet he'd been holding. "So, no galoshes, then."

"Afraid not," Oz said.

"Just as well," Xander said. "Wouldn't fit anyway." Xander plopped into a chair, put his feet up on the table and rested his head back in his intertwined hands, a wide grin on his face. "I think I've fallen in love."

"I thought you and Cordelia were past tense," Buffy said.

"Not Cordelia," Xander said. "Carnie or maybe Rave.

Although Lupa does have a special place in my heart. Hey, nothing against drummers, but that Nash is kinda standoffish, don't you think?"

"Xander, I think you're mistaking lust for love," Buffy said.

"Wouldn't be the first time," Willow added.

"Lust. Love," Xander said. "There's a very fine line when it comes to the heart of the seventeen-year-old male."

"Irrespective of Xander's affairs of the heart," Giles said, "we must identify as many of these victims as possible. Find out where they lived, where they went to school or work, when they disappeared. I'm convinced we'll find a pattern to determine where the killer or killers will strike next."

Willow veered toward the computer in the library. "Sounds like more research for Cybergal," she said. "Anything to take my mind off this 'forbidden history of Sunnydale' term paper."

"Hate to break this to you, Will," Xander said, "but the whole secret pit of gnawed human bones fits right into the forbidden section of Sunnydale's history."

"You're right," Willow said, pressing her palms against the sides of her head. "I'm doomed. How am I ever going to write this paper? It's not fair. I really do know too much."

Giles ran his hand through his hair. "Willow, I'm afraid you must draw upon the general reference volumes available on the history of Sunnydale."

"Forced to be a shill for the Chamber of Commerce," Willow said and sighed. "If only I could have temporary amnesia, at least until this history paper was finished. It happens all the time in the soaps. Not that I ever, you know, watch them."

Cordelia entered the library in time for the last comment. "What about the soaps? Are you talking about me and Troy?"

"No, Cordy," Xander said, "the whole world doesn't revolve around you and Dapper Dud."

"I'm surprised you're still here," Cordelia said. "I expected you to drop out of school by now to become a roadie for your precious Vyxn."

"Vixen?" Giles asked, confused. "Roadie? I'm afraid I'm not following."

"V-y-x-n," Buffy spelled. "All-girl band at the Bronze. You know, that whole Carnie, Rave, Lupa, Nash confusion earlier." Buffy gave Giles a conspiratorial look.

"Ah," Giles said, removing his eyeglasses as a way to avoid eye contact with Cordelia. "Thank you for clearing that up."

"What confusion?" Cordelia asked.

Willow spoke up. "Xander was just talking about . . . joining a fan club. And he couldn't decide which band member would be, um, the best."

"Tough decision," Oz remarked, playing along.

Cordelia cast a withering gaze at Xander. "Do I look like I even care whose poster he tapes to his bedroom wall?" Cordelia said with a dismissive wave of her hands. "Because I don't."

"Why should you? You have Troy to keep you warm at night," Xander said.

"That's—!"

Giles interrupted. "Look, this is all fascinating," he

said and, from his tone, it was clear he did not find it so. "But aren't we forgetting something?" He pointed to the pile of personal effects on the counter. "We need to find out about these victims before more people are killed."

"Oh, oh, I found one!" Willow said from in front of the computer. She had taken a couple wallets to the table with her and was running name searches cross-referenced with police reports. "Brandon Cortez was reported missing five days ago. Also a UC Sunnydale student. Last seen leaving a frat party. Reported missing by a roommate. Still no word on his whereabouts."

"That's because he's hereabouts," Xander said, flipping through the wallet. "New Mexico driver's license."

"Here's another one," Willow said. "Dave Sheppard. Reported missing six days ago by his parents." She looked up at them. "He went to Sunnydale High."

"I didn't know him," Buffy said.

"Young male victims thus far," Giles said. "There's a chance Xander and Oz might be at risk."

"Aren't we always at risk?" Xander asked. "As cardcarrying members of the Scooby Gang?"

"There is that, of course," Giles conceded. He had always been a little uncomfortable with the whole concept of the Slayer having a coterie of helpers. For a while, he'd thought the need for a Scooby Gang reflected negatively on his abilities as a Watcher. Still, he had to admit there was safety in numbers. Moreover, his Slayer, Buffy, was in the extraordinarily difficult position of warring with the supernatural right on top of the Hellmouth. If the average life of a Slayer was a short one, Buffy was truly fortunate to have such a devoted following to watch her back and, perhaps, improve the odds a bit. "Nevertheless, since neither of you are accustomed to being primary targets, you would do well to maintain a defensive posture."

"Best defense is a good offense," Oz said.

Xander enthused, "All we need is for Cyber Will to tell us which butts need some kickin'."

"This is hardly a laughing matter," Giles said.

"We have two choices," Xander said. "We can laugh . . . or we can run screaming in the night."

"Well, then, given the alternative—"

"See, Will, we have Giles on board for a major butt kick. Whatcha got for us?"

Willow shook her head. "Whatever is . . . *snacking* on the young men of Sunnydale," she said, "it doesn't leave any eyewitnesses behind."

Cordelia was looking through the personal effects still left on the counter. "What about all this stuff?"

"You're quite right, Cordelia," Giles said, nudging his glasses up the bridge of his nose. "After we glean what information we can from these items, we should return everything to the pit and report it to the police—anonymously, of course—so the families can be notified."

"I just meant it all looks too tacky to pawn or wear or anything," Cordelia said. "You think the families will actually want this stuff returned?"

Giles frowned at her startling lack of compassion. "I'm almost sure of it, Cordelia."

"No accounting for taste," Cordelia said, oblivious to the censure in his expression.

"The police?" Buffy said. "I can't wait to see what rational explanation they come up with to explain a pit of human bones."

"Wood chipper runs amok," Xander said. "Stray dogs hide bounty of bones."

"The existence of numerous victims would seem to point to a group of flesh-eaters, possibly a pack of ghouls, rather than a solitary predator."

"So I don't have to worry about that flame-headed hibachi demon you were so keen on?" Buffy asked, grinning.

"Rasselu demon," Giles corrected. "No, I should think not."

The class bell rang.

"Willow, perhaps it would be best if you resumed the search during a study period," Giles said. He gave the computer a wary look, cleared his throat and added, "Meanwhile, I'll have another look through the stacks for information about mounds of bones, mass graves, that sort of thing."

"There's a cheery thought," Cordelia said, rolling her eyes. She grabbed her books and headed toward the door. "I really have to stop coming in here."

"Not a problem," Xander called. "We're changing the locks."

But she was already gone.

Buffy slammed her locker shut, taking grim satisfaction in imprisoning her math book there. For the moment, she set aside regrets that the incarceration was only temporary. She would be lugging the thing home with her at the end of the day. It represented one of her problem classes.

"Willow," Buffy said. "I think it's time to wave the white flag over that yellow zone."

"Buffy, calculus isn't all that bad, I mean, if you stop and think about the practical applications and stuff."

"Practical applications?"

"Well, like, you know, figuring out the distance a crossbow bolt travels at a given velocity if— Okay, I lied. It is bad," Willow said, almost out of breath. "It's a bad, bad thing." She sighed. "There. Was I supportive?"

"The model of supportiveness. But another bad, bad thing is headed our way and the velocity is"— she whispered —"too late!"

"Well, well, well," Principal Snyder said. "If it isn't Ms. Summers." He made a point of checking the time on his wristwatch and then scribbling it down on a clipboard. There was something reptilian and sneaky about the way he patrolled the school halls, as if he were sure every student was up to no good and he was determined to finally catch every one of them in the act.

"Principal Snyder," Buffy said.

"I'm keeping my eye on you, Ms. Summers," he said. He looked down at the piece of paper on the clipboard. Buffy glimpsed a grid and lots of fine print, along with copious handwritten notes. "I have your complete class schedule here. If I'm not mistaken, you should have just finished calculus—but, hmm, no calculus textbook? How do you expect to excel if you forget the proper texts? Or did you just skip that pesky calculus class? That would certainly explain it."

"Explain what?" Buffy asked.

"Why calculus has been designated as one of your trouble zones by Mrs. Burzak," Snyder said, positively glowing over Buffy's difficulties.

"Look, Snyder—" Buffy said, omitting his title in her exasperation. Just how far did Burzak's network of scholastic spies extend? *Why can't that woman just leave me alone?* "The book is in my locker. I was in the class. Believe me, I will live with the memories."

"A concerned student would stay after class," Snyder said. "Ask for extra credit assignments. Then again, I never counted Buffy Summers among my concerned students."

"On the contrary," Willow said. "Buffy was just asking if I would sleep over her house for a late-night tutoring session."

"I . . . was?"

"You were."

"I was," Buffy said, with a "so, there!" nod to Snyder.

"She'll be burning the midnight oil," Willow said. "How's that for being a concerned student?"

Snyder nodded, conceding the advantage, for now. "But don't think this means I won't be keeping track of you, Ms. Summers, from morning bell till school dismissal. Mrs. Burzak has identified you as a troubled student and asked for my help in setting you on the straight and narrow. I'd hate to see you . . . slip up and face expulsion again." By the excited gleam in his eye, Buffy knew that was exactly what he'd like to see happen.

When they were alone again, Buffy said, "Does it ever bother you that we and Principal Snyder are members of the same species?"

"We're on the Hellmouth," Willow said. "So we can't really be sure."

"This is true," Buffy said. "Thanks for bailing me out, Willow, but you don't have to—"

Willow held up a hand. "My overnight bag is already packed."

"But what about your history paper?" Buffy asked. "I know that whole honesty thing is bothering you. Not that that's a bad thing."

"Actually, I think it's giving me hives," Willow said, unconsciously rubbing her arms. "I feel like a fraud, forced to write a completely false history of Sunnydale. Where's my journalistic integrity?"

"Willow, you're not a journalist."

"Theoretical journalistic integrity."

"Don't think of it that way," Buffy said. "Think of it as a creative writing assignment."

"The conscience is a prickly little beast," Willow said. "It jabs you and pokes you and puts soft, lumpy things in your milk and won't let you get any sleep." She sighed. "At least it's only an academic dilemma eating away at me. Oz and Xander could be supernatural specials of the day. I'll look out for Oz, but what about Xander?"

"Cordelia will probably hang around just to make sure he stays miserable."

"Oh, but Cordelia has Troy now," Willow said. Buffy watched as her friend got a dreamy look in her eyes. "You know, he plays Zack Garner on *Wanderlust*. See, Zack's a rebel rich kid who has a way with horses and with the women. He's—oh—I mean, not that I've ever watched it, really, I just read somewhere or heard—"

She bit her lip, looked chagrined. "Sometimes my mother talks."

"Hmm," Buffy said, grinning. "Maybe I should be taping."

"Really?" Willow said, excitement bubbling up again. "If you want, I could lend— I mean, yes, you could tape."

"So . . . what were we talking about?"

"Was it horses?" Willow asked innocently.

"Xander," Buffy said.

"Oh, right," Willow said. "Xander."

"Xander is smitten," Buffy said. "Which means, he'll stay put at the Bronze. At least for a couple days. Maybe that's the safest place for him to be until we figure this out."

Chapter 7

Buffy walked through her house, calling, "Mom?"

She entered the kitchen, expecting her mother to be there, maybe flipping through department store ads or doing the crossword puzzle. But the kitchen was empty. As she placed her backpack on the kitchen table, her foot crunched on something and she looked down to see a broken mug, pieces of ceramic scattered across the tile floor. It was the sand-colored Philadelphia Art Museum mug her mother had been sipping coffee from that morning.

"Mom?" Buffy called. No answer.

Then she noticed it. On the table, beside her backpack, was a playing card, the jack of clubs.

Footfalls on the basement stairs, getting closer.

Buffy slipped a wooden stake from her bag and stalked toward the basement door, not making a sound.

The basement door was open several inches. She should have noticed it when she came into the house. *Careless,* she thought. Now she waited beside the door, poised, ready to attack whoever or whatever had invaded her home. The door swung open. Buffy raised the stake.

Her mother gasped, almost dropping the dustpan and brush she had carried up from the basement shelf. "Buffy!"

"Mom!" Buffy said, her heart racing. She'd been way too close to staking her own mother.

"You scared me to death," Joyce Summers said, breathless.

"The feeling's mutual," Buffy said. "I . . . I saw the broken mug on the floor and assumed—"

"That I dropped it while emptying the dishwasher?"

"Which is . . . also a reasonable assumption." She followed her mother into the kitchen, held the dustpan at an angle as her mother swept the ceramic debris toward her. "So, I wanted to let you know that Willow's coming over tonight, if that's okay. Kind of a calculus tutoring sleep-over."

"That's good, Buffy," Joyce said. "I'm glad you're taking the initiative with these problem subjects. By the way, I had a visitor stop by this morning."

"Not my guidance counselor. She's—"

"No. It was a man. A strange man."

"Strange, how?" Buffy asked, her irritation replaced with a new sense of alarm.

"It was the oddest thing," Joyce said, recalling the incident. "He said he was a dealer in Sumerian antiquities, said that an associate gave him my name, that he thought I might be interested in what he had in his briefcase."

"So, what did he have? Really old pots and pans?"

"Nothing."

"Nothing?" Buffy said. "I don't follow. He said you'd be interested in nothing?"

"That's the odd part," Joyce said, laughing. "He was absentminded and, apparently, forgot to pack anything in his briefcase. He just came into the house for a minute and then his case was completely—"

"Wait a minute," Buffy said, alarmed. "You *invited* him in?"

"Yes, but I know what you're thinking," Joyce replied. "That a . . . a vampire has to be invited in. But Buffy, this was broad daylight. He squinted a little, but he was obviously walking around on a sunny day without bursting into flames. I think I would have noticed that."

"Did this guy have a name?" Buffy dumped the pieces of the museum mug into the kitchen trash can.

"Well, he left his card, if you can call it that," Joyce said. She picked up the jack of clubs playing card. "He apologized for forgetting his business cards as well, so he wrote his number on the back of this card. I told him to stop by the gallery later, but he never showed or called."

"Let me see that," Buffy said. She read the name on the back of the card, L'taire—*sounds French?*—and the telephone number. She picked up the phone and dialed the number.

After several rings, a telephone operator's voice spoke. "The cellular customer is unavailable."

Buffy hung up, then dialed Giles's home number. As usual, Giles sounded as if he'd had his nose buried in a dusty old book and still hadn't pulled it all the way out.

"Oh, Buffy, hello. I'm glad you called. I was just pursuing the possibility that there might be some other mechanism for the removal of the flesh from the bones. An acid bath, maybe. Or the victims could have been boiled until the flesh—"

"You need to get out more, Giles," Buffy said. "Listen, my—"

"Oh, and a Mrs. Burzak asked me to talk to you about some . . . red zones?"

Buffy sighed. Et tu, *Giles?* "We can talk about my commando counselor some other time, Giles. The reason I called—"

"You called—? Oh, yes, quite right. Do go on, then."

"My mother had an odd visitor today."

"An encyclopedia salesman, perhaps?"

"No," Buffy said, ignoring Giles's dry attempt at humor. "He said he was a museum guy. But after my mother *invited* him into the house, his bags were empty and he just left."

"Ah," Giles said. "But you said *today*. In daylight?"

"This morning," Buffy said, her shoulders slumping. "I know. Obviously not a vampire. But strange." Buffy explained how the man had presented himself to get inside the house.

"Nothing in his case, you say?" Giles was silent for a moment. "Either he is incredibly forgetful or the sole purpose of his visit was a pretext to gain entry into your house."

"That's what worries me," Buffy said, flipping the playing card over in her hand. "Jack of clubs . . ."

"What was that?"

"He also forgot his business cards," Buffy explained. "So he left his phone number on a playing card."

"A playing card? Hmm . . . now why should that seem familiar?"

"You're the Watcher," Buffy said. "I save the Double Jeopardy round for you."

"I'm sure it will come to me," Giles said. "Bring the card with you tomorrow."

Lupa paced in the Vyxn dressing room, repeatedly slapping a wireless microphone in her palm. With each impact, her palm turned a pale shade of green before reverting to a normal flesh tone. "Our first set was a little rough."

"We got them right where we want them," Nash said, ignoring the comment. She spun a drumstick in her hand before striking it against the back of a chair.

That's the problem, Lupa thought. They had a captive audience, ripe for the picking, and they were so close to the Slayer, prepared to strike at any moment . . . yet Lupa held back. As troupe leader, she must give the order, to go for broke, as the humans said. Still, she hesitated.

Rave crossed her arms and leaned against the wall, shaking her head. "We wouldn't have waited this long if you weren't so worried about the Slayer."

"I'm not worried about her," Lupa said.

"Prove it," Carnie said, a little too boldly for Lupa's taste. The redhead's appetite was always the first to resurface. Their need was putting all of them on edge and just now it was manifesting as a challenge to her authority. "Choose someone tonight."

"Me, I'd choose Xander," Nash said.

"Sure," Carnie agreed. "He's cute." She examined her intricately lacquered fingernails, flexed her fingers, then extended them and watched as the skin turned a mottled green and her fingernails became coarse and yellow, with sharp, hooked points. In their natural form, her nails bore more resemblance to animal claws or hooves than they did to frail human fingernails. She closed her fist and opened it again, revealing her human fingers and fingernails once more. "Let's do him."

Lupa shook her head. "No. He's friend to the Slayer. He'll have other uses."

"Then pick somebody else, Lupa," Rave said. "We're hungry."

Lupa nodded. While Carnie and Nash were usually slaves to their hunger at the expense of common sense, Rave was the only one—other than Lupa herself—who could think beyond her next meal. In a bold move to make the troupe strong again, Lupa had brought them to the Slayer's hunting grounds. Then she had been overly cautious in postponing their regular feeding. *What sense was there in confronting the Slayer in a hunger-weakened state?* The time had come to follow one bold move with another. "Tonight," Lupa declared. "We feed tonight."

Waiting for Vyxn to begin their second set, Xander sipped soda at a round table in the Bronze, accompanied by Oz and Troy Douglas. While Xander wore a checked shirt over khakis, and Oz wore a green three-button shirt and dark pants, Troy wore a slate gray two-piece designer suit that had probably cost more than Xander's entire wardrobe. Xander examined the crowd and saw that it was predominantly male and figured Vyxn's word of mouth rep must be spreading like wildfire. *Only a few nights left,* Xander thought. *Might as well make the most of it. Besides, who knows how far away the band's next stop might be?*

"So, no Willow tonight, Oz?"

"History paper, then Buffy's for a tutoring sleepover," Oz said, then nipped at a pretzel.

"Gotta admire that dedication," Xander said, turning his attention to Troy. "What about you, Zit Man? Finally manage to slip Cordelia's leash?"

Troy chuckled. "I think I preferred it when you called me Pimple Boy." He grabbed a pretzel. "Anyway, we're gonna hook up later."

"So you two are getting serious?"

"We're just old friends catching up," Troy replied. "Besides, I won't be around town much longer."

"That's good—I mean—"

The crowd cheered, rising to its feet as Vyxn took the stage again. Thunderous applause filled the Bronze. Carnie began the set by playing a mournful bass riff, which was joined by a slow, steady drumbeat from Nash. Lupa cupped a wireless mike close to her mouth, tilted her head and sang softly.

"The night weeps for you,
the rain is falling down,
And I am hollow now
On the bus out of town . . ."

The song was called "Bus Stop" and the band had played it each night, yet it still filled Xander with the same vague sense of longing, that he was missing something important and could regain if only he tried hard enough. Before Lupa finished singing the first verse, Xander forgot what he had been so upset about. He settled down in his chair and listened raptly.

Several songs into the set, Xander, Oz and Troy were all bobbing their heads in time to the drumbeat, completely unaware of each other or their surroundings. Only Vyxn seemed to matter, but that seemed perfectly natural.

"Pathetic much!" Cordelia said, interrupting another mournful ballad.

Troy shook his head, clearing the cobwebs. "Oh—uh, Cordelia, glad you're here."

Oz looked up at her. "Hey."

"Hi, Cordy," Xander said, but turned his attention back to the stage.

Cordelia Chase stood with her hands indignantly planted on her hips. "Xander, I knew you were hopeless. But, Oz? I thought, musically at least, you'd have better taste. And, Troy"—she shook her head for emphasis—"you're the biggest disappointment. I thought you were a little more mature than these hormonally charged guys."

"I . . . I was just waiting to call—" Troy's mistake was a sidelong glance at the stage during the middle of his explanation.

"Save it. I see your brain is already overloaded."

She was gone and Troy felt he should follow her, but Lupa had just finished her song and was at that moment pointing her finger at him. "Time for a dedication," she said and stepped off the stage. She leaned over, revealing a startling amount of cleavage. With her face next to his, he noticed that her skin was smooth and utterly dry, though he smelled a musky scent coming off of her. "Tell me your name," she whispered in his ear.

"Troy," he whispered right back, felt compelled to do so. "Troy Douglas."

"Ah, Troy," she said, so soft that only he could hear her. "What a lovely name. You know what I want you to do, Troy, I want you to . . ." Her words then flowed so fast he could no longer consciously distinguish one from the next and he wasn't meant to, though deep in his mind, he understood the commands.

Xander watched, annoyed that Lupa had decided to give Troy the dedication treatment. First Troy moved on Cordy, now he was monopolizing Vyxn's attention. He watched as Troy first smiled, then seemed to stare off into space before finally just nodding twice, slowly. Lupa stepped away from him. Xander thought she'd probably given Troy her phone number for after the show.

Lupa retook the stage, swaying her hips hypnotically before turning slowly to face the crowd. "This is the last song of our next to last set. It's called 'Tender Heart' and it's dedicated to Troy, the gorgeous guy sitting right here up front and dressed for success."

That's laying it on a bit thick, Xander thought, disgruntled. He couldn't enjoy the song as much as he would have liked to, mostly because he kept looking at Troy to see how he was reacting to his dedication song. Stone-faced, is how Xander would have described his reaction. However, just as the song was fading, Troy became agitated. He looked over at Xander and Oz.

"I need to find Cordelia," Troy said. "Apologize for ignoring her."

"An apology." Xander nodded his head. "Oh, that will definitely make her fall into your arms."

Troy shrugged, as if to say it was worth a shot. He stood and slipped between a few tables to get to the door.

Lupa watched him go, pouted to show her disappointment and then gave the crowd a little wave. "We're gonna grab a quick snack," Lupa said. "Don't run away on us!" The crowd laughed, cheering and clapping as if the mere suggestion was the ultimate in absurdity. "See ya in ten, guys!"

Xander looked at Oz after the band had left the stage. "You staying for the last set, Oz Man?" Xander felt wiped out after the band had walked offstage. Looking around, he saw that many of the guys who had been cheering a moment ago, looked as if they were waiting for a second wind. An exhilarating show that exhausted the audience. *That was a good thing,* he thought. *Right?*

"Wouldn't miss it," Oz said. He picked up the basket on the table and turned it upside down, surprised to find it empty. "We're gonna need more pretzels."

As the cool night air washed over Troy Douglas, reviving him slightly, he stood looking from left to right and couldn't remember why he'd left the Bronze in the first place. Something had seemed urgent a moment or two ago, but it had completely slipped his mind. He stuffed his hands into his trouser pockets and sighed heavily. He recalled that he'd meant to call Cordelia earlier, but it was probably too late for that now. But there was something about Cordelia . . .

"Troy . . ."

The voice was barely a whisper. He almost imagined the sound had been conjured by his imagination.

"Troy . . ."

He looked from left to right. Nobody was hanging outside the Bronze. *So where had the voice come from?* he wondered.

"*Troy Douglas . . .*" the voice whispered, seemingly audible now, a woman's voice, definitely.

"Who's there?" he asked. The voice had come from the right side of the Bronze. He started walking in that direction. *Could it be Cordelia?* Maybe she was waiting for him out here, in the dark. "Cordelia? Cordelia, is that you?"

He neared the corner of the building and peered around the side, saw a figure standing there, in silhouette. "*Come . . .*"

A woman. She seemed taller than Cordelia, standing near a battle-scarred Dumpster, which was hardly romantic and certainly not the type of location Cordelia would have chosen for a rendezvous. He was, however, accustomed to female fans of "Wanderlust" confronting him in the oddest places for an autograph or even a kiss. One young woman had followed him into an airport men's room to tell him she was his number one fan.

Another woman stepped out from behind the Dumpster, followed by a third and a fourth. They fanned out but did not approach. "*Come to us, Troy Douglas,*" the first one said in a voice that made him shiver. Something about that voice seemed familiar . . . and the way she spoke his name, like a caress inside his mind. Before he was completely aware of his actions, he found himself walking toward the women.

"Hello, ladies," he said. Still thinking fans or groupies had found him out in Sunnydale.

They were anything but ladies.

Willow Rosenberg had finally tossed up her hands in defeat over her history term paper. *Defeat is too definitive a statement. Let's call it a strategic retreat for the evening.* She simply felt like a fraud parroting Chamber of Commerce statistics when she knew the truth behind the history of Sunnydale, behind the Hellmouth. Even though she'd told Oz she would head over to Buffy's house after putting in some time on the paper, she had waved the white flag earlier than she would have predicted. So it was too soon to drop in on Buffy, who was probably out somewhere with Angel anyway, looking for another cache of human bones or introducing some newly risen vampire to Mr. Pointy.

Instead, she found herself approaching the Bronze. She figured Oz would be in there with Xander. Oz had tried to hide it, but he was obviously attracted to Vyxn— well, vixens—with their wild hair and seductive looks and the distressed strips of leather they called stage costumes. She doubted Oz's interest was in Vyxn's meager musical talents. To Willow, they represented everything she was not and knowing that Oz might be attracted to their brash sex appeal made her feel a little inadequate. She couldn't compete with them on any level . . . well, except for maybe nailing down an obscure Internet search topic in record time. But Willow was pretty sure *that* talent wouldn't impress a whole lot of guys. *Actually*, she thought, *it would probably intimidate them*. Guys generally weren't real keen on feeling intimidated.

Though Oz always made her feel special, somehow this wiggly little doubt had wormed its way into her subconscious. Now she could only think of the things she was *not*. Oz had had other girlfriends before her and she assumed she compared favorably to them since, obviously, they weren't in the picture anymore. Still, Oz was her first boyfriend, which wasn't much of a relationship history at all. How could she know why one relationship ended while another endured? Maybe Oz saw something in Vyxn that she was lacking, something that would make him realize Willow Rosenberg wasn't all that great, after all. Insecurity had a way of feeding on itself.

She figured dropping in for a surprise visit would get Oz's attention, maybe show him she could be the spontaneous girl if she wanted and she was pretty sure guys liked spontaneity. *That is kind of exciting, isn't it?*

But she never made it past the Vyxn sandwich board. Before she could enter the Bronze, she heard a strange sound from around the side of the building. It sounded like a scuffle and she thought some high school guys might be fighting over some real or imagined insult. Yet Willow was a veteran of all—well, a disgustingly and frighteningly assorted sample of all—the Hellmouth had to spew out at the people of Sunnydale, so she approached cautiously. As an official member of the Slayerettes, she was embarrassed to admit she was prepared to turn tail and run at the slightest sign of anything supernatural. "Discretion can be the better part of valor," she whispered to herself. Still, she had faced many evil and icky things since joining Buffy's inner circle and had managed to maintain a semblance of courage and dignity throughout.

She peered cautiously around the corner and saw them, three of them, in silhouette, crouching over a guy lying on the ground. Her first thought was that he—who-ever he was—had had too much to drink and had gone around the side of the building, accompanied by his con-cerned friends, to be sick. But that impression was fleet-ing. She realized all the crouchers were female, while the crouchee was definitely a guy. That was unusual enough in itself. But the clincher was the sounds the crouchers were making—wet, snuffling noises, like pigs at a trough. *Or wild dogs with a fresh kill.*

She'd seen more than enough to know it was too late to help the guy but not too late to run before she became a second course. She stepped back carefully and her heel scraped against a stone. The woman nearest her, with her back turned, whipped her head around and the wild mane of red hair immediately brought to Willow's mind the image of Vyxn's bass player, Carnie. Only her face was a mottled green and her teeth were two or three rows deep, gnarled and intertwined and covered with gore, as were her coarse, hooked fingernails. Beyond her, his face partly in shadow and partly streaked with his own blood, lay Troy Douglas.

Willow easily identified another of the green-faced predators by her white Mohawk-ponytail as the lead gui-tarist, Rave. And opposite her, judging by the spiky hair and spiked collar, the drummer, Nash. Which begged one important question. "Sorry to not eat and run, but—"

As Willow took another step backward, she felt a rush of air and heard the impact of thick-soled boots strike down behind her. She froze as clawed hands clamped down on her shoulders. Willow looked back at the formerly missing lead singer, Lupa. She still had wild black hair, shaved at the sides of her head, but her skin was a mottled green, her eyes a glowing, feral yellow and her mouth filled with two, maybe three rows of gnarled fangs with bits of raw flesh strung between them. Willow felt her knees go wobbly.

"She's afraid," Lupa called to the others. "Too afraid."

Willow wasn't sure what she meant by that comment until Rave said, "Guess she's not the Slayer, after all."

"Me, I say we kill her," Nash called.

Lupa's right hand closed around Willow's throat, the claws beginning to dig into her flesh. Willow wondered if she could somehow scream before Lupa tore her throat out. Not that it would matter all that much to Willow, she'd be too dead to be rescued, anyway. "No," Lupa said, suddenly easing the grip she had on Willow's throat. "She may not be the Slayer, but I sense something powerful in her. She might have her uses."

Willow struggled to break free, but she just wasn't strong enough. Lupa spun her around bodily, one hand's sharp claws digging painfully into Willow's shoulder while the other set of claws clamped over Willow's mouth.

"Do you want to die this instant?" Willow shook her head vigorously. "Good. Because if you scream or try to run I'll rip your throat out. Understood?" Willow nodded just as assertively.

"What are you thinking?" Carnie hissed.

"She's wasting time, I say," Nash grumbled. "Kill her already."

"Rave knows what I have in mind," Lupa said.

Rave nodded. "Well, we have needed a keyboard player ever since Viola's untimely end."

"You'd make her one of us?" Carnie asked, mulling over the idea.

"I have a sense about these things," Lupa said. "I think she'd make a perfect little ghoul. Besides, until the transformation, she's prime Slayer bait." Lupa looked down at Willow, lifted her claws away from her mouth. "Your decision."

Ghouls! Willow thought nervously, Giles had thought the bones might be the work of ghouls. *We thought they were hiding, but they were right in front of us the whole time!* "You can't—turn people into ghouls?"

"Ladies only," Lupa said. "One little ceremony and you're in. You'd join the band, learn to play keyboards, see the world, have lots of groupies and you'd get to eat some of them."

"But then I'd miss out on college," Willow stammered. Vampires could turn humans into vampires, so it made perfect sense that ghouls could somehow turn humans into ghouls.

Lupa's hand closed around her throat again. "You'll miss college if I have to tear your throat out. Quickly now, what's your decision?"

"Wait—wait! This is a really big decision, since my

being a ghoul would mean skipping college, leaving home and eating of human flesh—and there's no way that can be kosher—and, oh, I'm guessing eternal damnation. Do you—uh—mind if I, um, sleep on it and get back to you?"

Lupa tightened her grip. "Not at all."

CHAPTER 8

"**M**om, did Willow call?"

"No, dear," Joyce Summers said, momentarily looking up from the silk flowers she was arranging on a table in the foyer.

Buffy sat at the kitchen table and stared at the telephone on the wall. She'd been over an hour late getting back from an uneventful patrol with Angel—no bones, caches, or creatures wanting to go bump in the night—and thought for sure Willow would have phoned by now. It was possible she'd forgotten their plans, but that was very un-Willow-y. Buffy called Willow's mother and found out that Willow had indeed left home with plans to stay overnight at Buffy's, but had mentioned something about seeing Oz first.

Buffy tried Oz's number next, figuring boyfriend-

change-of-plans happened. But Oz hadn't seen her since
school let out. He said he'd been at the Bronze with
Xander and Troy, at least until Troy rushed out after an
irritated Cordelia. "Willow never showed," Oz said. "But
I wasn't expecting her . . ."

"Hmm."

"What's happened?"

"I don't know," she said. "Maybe nothing. Let's not
jump to panic-button-pushing mode yet. It's still early. I
have a few more calls to make. If I come up empty, we'll
all meet at Giles's place."

Rupert Giles was holding a cup of tea but it had been
awhile since Buffy last saw him take a sip. She supposed
just holding the cup helped him think. He was staring at
the jack of clubs playing card she'd handed him even
while the others discussed the last time they'd seen Willow. Cordelia had been the last to arrive. Buffy had almost decided against calling her, but it was possible
Cordelia had had contact with Willow and it was better
to leave no stone unturned. Fortunately, Cordelia had
shown enough concern for Willow's welfare to join them
here, even if she had made some comment about lost
beauty sleep before she was three steps through the door.

"So Willow had no idea you were at the Bronze?"
Buffy asked Oz, who was too nervous to sit down. His
hands were stuffed into his pockets, his head down, deep
in thought, probably replaying his entire day as it related
to Willow, in his mind.

"Reasonable assumption," Oz said. "Not many other
places to hang."

"Cordelia, you didn't see her at all?"

"I was only there for a minute," Cordelia said. "Just long enough to see that Troy had joined *their*"—she pointed in Xander's and Oz's general direction—"drooling club. They wouldn't have noticed Willow if she'd been dancing on one of the pool tables."

"That's not fair," Oz said, frowning and irritated.

"I'm guessing Troy's apology was a big old waste of time," Xander said.

"What apology?"

"He ran out after you," Xander said.

"Well, not right after," Oz said. What he didn't say was that Troy hadn't felt all that guilty until the end of Vyxn's dedication song.

"I never saw him after I left." Cordelia sighed, then added wistfully, "He promised me a screen test with the producers of *Wanderlust*. But I wouldn't give him the satisfaction now."

"Wait a minute, Cordelia," Giles said, finally looking up from the jack of clubs. "You're saying that Troy is missing as well?"

"Well, I haven't talked to him."

"Giles, are you thinking—?" Buffy said.

Giles nodded. "He fits the pattern."

"What pattern?" Cordelia asked. "Hormonally charged guys?"

"The hormonally-charged-guys-who-get-eaten-by-ghouls pattern," Xander said, catching on.

Giles came out from behind his kitchen counter. "We must be sure. Try to get in touch with him."

Cordelia nodded. "I'll try his mother's number," she

said, taking her cell phone out of her pocketbook. "But if he answers, I'm hanging up. I refuse to talk to him." She waited while the phone rang, mouthed "his mother" to the group, then asked if Troy was available. She hung up the phone. "She hasn't seen him since he left for the Bronze."

"And he was last seen leaving the Bronze," Giles said.

"Where Willow may have been going when she disappeared," Xander added.

"Troy *and* Willow," Cordelia said. "You don't suppose they could have . . . run off together?"

"Hardly," Giles replied, not giving the idea a moment's consideration.

"You're right. Willow is definitely not his type."

Giles sat down on the sofa. "It's possible whatever has been attacking these other young men also attacked Troy after he left the Bronze."

"Young men?" Cordelia said. "Willow may dress a little frumpy, but she's not a guy."

"She could have witnessed . . . whatever it was," Buffy suggested, changing what she was about to say when she noticed Oz's distressed expression.

"We should look for clues at the Bronze," Giles said.

"Xander, Oz, did you notice anything unusual after Troy left?" Buffy asked.

"Let's see. . . . He left after the band's second set," Xander said. "Place was quiet, kinda subdued during the break, music on house speakers, some guys playing pool. Band finished up with a third set. Just a few songs." Xander shook his head. "Nothing unusual."

"Still, the Bronze is the last place where anyone saw Troy," Giles said. "I believe we should go there and look for something, anything, that might tell us what happened. I'll round up some torches—er, flashlights." Giles was about to place the playing card on the coffee table when he paused and looked up at Buffy. "I just remembered."

"Remembered what?"

"Just a minute." Giles walked over to a magazine rack that was home to several folded newspapers. He flipped through them, then pointed at an article on the front page, skimming aloud. "There! 'Violent altercation at a disreputable establishment. EZ Rider. Several killed, others injured.' Aha! A playing card was left on the body of a biker chap known as . . . Warhammer."

"You think the French guy who talked to my mom is related?"

"French guy?" Giles asked. "Oh, the name. S.O. L'taire. Solitaire."

"Giles, is this any time to be thinking of card games?" Xander asked.

"Solitaire," Giles repeated. "I recall reading in the old texts something about an unusual vampire who called himself Solitaire."

"Vampire? This Solitaire guy showed up at Buffy's house in the morning," Xander reminded him.

"Yes, a bit problematic, that," Giles said, pushing his glasses up on his nose.

"Sounds more like a con man," Xander said. "An incompetent con man, I'll admit. But not a creature of the night."

"What about him asking to be invited into the house?" Cordelia said.

"Con man code of ethics?" Oz ventured.

"There's something wiggy about him," Buffy said.

"Quite right," Giles said. "I think it best we erred on the side of caution. Buffy, you and the others check the Bronze. I'll stop by your house and perform the spell to uninvite this Solitaire. Just to be safe."

"Sounds like a plan," Buffy said. "We'll pick up Angel on the way to the Bronze." Xander gave her a quick look at the mention of Angel's name. She realized he was thinking of the last time they had had to perform the un-invite spell on Buffy's house, during the time Angel had lost his soul and reverted to his evil Angelus incarnation.

Giles closed the door behind them and then hurriedly gathered his things in a worn, black satchel: an old, leather-bound volume containing the proper incantation, the necessary ingredients for the spell, along with an extra vial of holy water, a metal cross, a wooden stake and a crossbow with several quarrels. He didn't expect to run into a vampire on the way to the Summers's residence but, as a Watcher, he saw no harm in preparing for that possibility.

A quick rap of knuckles against his door. *Probably Xander,* Giles thought, and wondered what he could have forgotten. He dropped the satchel on the sofa and opened the door. "Yes—what is it?"

Nobody was there.

Giles leaned out and instantly a hand gripped his throat so tightly he couldn't breathe. The tall, muscular man stepped out of the shadows at the side of the door without easing his grip. He had close-cropped blond hair and a deeply lined, pale face with broad cheekbones and thin, cruel lips. He wore a black overcoat over a red leather vest.

"I thought they'd never leave," he said. "Now invite me in, Watcher."

Giles realized his options were limited at the moment. He had to buy himself some time. "By . . . by all means, do come in," he croaked.

The man shoved him backward, causing Giles to lose his balance. Giles exaggerated his clumsiness a bit in order to clutch at the satchel on the sofa. He hadn't zipped it shut yet and could just see the butt of the stake resting near the top.

Giles watched as the intruder slammed the door shut, then leaned against it. When the man took a playing card—a ten of diamonds—from a vest pocket and began to pick under his fingernails with it, Giles realized who he was. *Sometimes knowledge is power.* "I demand to know who you are," Giles said. He clutched at the edge of the satchel flap, hoping it would appear to be a nervous tic.

"Buffy Summers must be an extraordinary young woman," Solitaire said.

"I'm afraid I don't know what you're talking about," Giles said. His hand had slipped over the butt of the stake. Slowly, he inched it up into his hand, hidden from Solitaire's view.

"I must admit I was quite impressed when I heard rumors of a Slayer who had defeated the Order of Taraka," Solitaire said. He was flicking his finger over the edge of the playing card now. "I couldn't help but wonder if she was up to a greater challenge," he said. "Me, for instance."

"Who are you?" Giles asked, turning the stake over in his hand so he'd be ready to strike with it when the moment presented itself.

"If you don't know who I am by now, Watcher," Solitaire said as he stepped away from the door, "I will be greatly disappointed."

Giles swallowed hard, tightened his grip on the stake even as he felt his palm become moist with sweat.

"Here's a clue," Solitaire said and snarled, flashing a pair of long fangs at Giles as his brow and snout furrowed in the characteristic manner of a vampire. He moved another step closer.

"I do know what . . . what you are," Giles said. "Just not why you're here, exactly."

"I want you to pass along a message to your Slayer—"

"I have a message—" Giles lunged with the stake, striking down at Solitaire's chest. His wrist was caught in a vice-grip, the point of the stake quivering mere inches from Solitaire's chest. Giles strained, with all his strength. The grip on his wrist tightened. He heard bones snap. Shooting pain blinded him for an instant.

"Do I have your attention now?" Solitaire asked, forcing Giles down to his knees with the pressure he exerted on the Watcher's damaged wrist.

Giles grimaced. "A . . . a message, you say?"

"Yes," Solitaire said. He dropped the ten of diamonds at Giles's knees, then pried the stake out of the Watcher's numb fingers with his free hand. Solitaire flipped the stake in his hand so that he held it by the narrow end.

"Tell your Slayer she'll be dying to make my acquaintance."

"How terribly original of you," Giles said, then gritted his teeth against the pain.

"This isn't original—" Solitaire snarled again and whipped the butt of the stake against the Watcher's head. "—but effective."

Giles felt himself falling away. The darkness rose up to claim him.

After searching outside the Bronze for a while, Xander finally asked the obvious question. "What exactly are we looking for?"

Of course, the Bronze had been closed by the time they arrived. Only feeble street lamps cast wan light and shadow on the front and sides of the building, more a deterrent to arsonists than a source of real illumination. They had arrived with three flashlights and a lot of ground to cover. Oz took one flashlight, preferring to search alone, while Buffy paired off with Angel, which left Xander and Cordelia working together in an uneasy détente.

"I don't know, Xander," Buffy said, finally responding to Xander's question. "Footprints?"

"On asphalt?" he asked.

"Matchbooks," Cordelia suggested. "They always find matchbooks in the movies. Leads them to the nightclub where the killer hangs out."

Xander glanced at Oz who, fortunately, hadn't been listening, then glared at Cordelia. "What? What did I say?" she asked.

"We're already at the club," Buffy said patiently. "We

need something to lead us back to—back to whoever or whatever is involved in this."

Xander wandered back toward the Dumpster located at the side of the Bronze. Not wanting to be left alone in the dark, Cordelia followed him. Shortly after they had arrived, Xander had flipped open the heavy metal lid and cast his flashlight beam into the smelly debris. He had been so relieved not to see a body sprawled in the beer-soaked cardboard and lumpy garbage that he had looked no further. Now he had returned to his starting point. "I don't suppose anyone has scuba gear handy?" No one said anything. "Okay, I'll settle for a clothespin for my nose." He shrugged. "Didn't think so." He handed Cordelia the flashlight, then hoisted himself onto the edge of the Dumpster.

"You're not actually getting in there, are you?" Cordelia asked.

"Are you volunteering?"

"That is totally disgusting." Cordelia shuddered.

"No, he's right," Oz said, having stepped up beside them when he saw what Xander had in mind.

When Oz grabbed the edge of the Dumpster to lift himself up, Xander held up a hand already coated with coffee grounds. "I got it, Oz. Not enough room in here for both of us and all the . . . leavin's. Just shine your light down here if you would. Maybe it will scare away the rats."

Cordelia jumped back a step, glanced down nervously at her open-toed shoes. "Rats! Yuck—there's rats? I hate rats. I wouldn't even be here if it weren't for Troy. As much as I hate to admit it, you and your Scooby Gang have the best chance of finding him"—she glanced at

Oz—"and Willow, of course. Wouldn't forget about Willow. It's just—I really hate rats."

"Not real fond of 'em myself, Cordy," Xander said.

Giles groaned and struggled up from the darkness that tugged at him like sleep long denied. His good hand fumbled at his scalp, which had been cut. The surrounding area was sticky with half-congealed blood, one eye glued shut. His other hand and wrist throbbed painfully. The pain was probably what had roused him. At first he couldn't remember where he was or what had happened to him.

His hand flopped down to his chest and found something smooth and rectangular there. He raised it to his good eye. A playing card. And it all came back to him. Solitaire. His wrist. The message for Buffy. Then the emphatic blow to the head. Giles sat up, felt only slightly dizzy, so climbed to his feet, using the wall for support. He must drive to the Bronze, warn Buffy. While standing seemed precarious, when he started toward the door, his legs felt as if they were on stilts, his feet so far below him. *Definitely in no condition to drive,* he thought. He staggered to the telephone and oddly remembered that parents on airplanes were instructed to put oxygen masks on themselves first so they did not pass out before they could place masks on their children. Odd . . . he had no children. He dialed 911. "Thank you, yes, this is, ah, Rupert Giles. I believe I may be in need of medical attention. Yes, it's—" When his own address did not come immediately to mind, he thought it rather clever of him to refer to his driver's license for the information. He'd been banged around quite a bit and was probably suffering from a concussion on top of all that, so minor victories were to be cherished.

Oxygen, he thought, while he waited for help to arrive. He stared at the telephone numbers, grasping at a thought that eluded him. "Ah—Buffy, yes." He checked the time and decided she would still be at the Bronze, unreachable. Cordelia had a cell phone, but he couldn't recall the number if he had ever known it. Instead he dialed Buffy's home number. He'd probably wake Joyce, but this was something of an emergency and she would—would. . . . The darkness was rising again, too quickly. He felt the telephone receiver slip from his grasp and drop to the floor, although the sound was oddly muffled. Darkness enfolded him, pulled him down with one last, fading thought . . . *oxygen.*

If Xander were a pig, he'd probably be delirious by now. He'd rooted his way through every last beer bottle and soda can, the odd banana peel and mound of potato chip crumbs, goopy bread and rolls, rancid chunks of meat and sticky eggshells, soggy cardboard, soiled tissues and clumps of cigarette ashes and the ever popular wads of gum. Somebody had dumped several cartons of Chinese food into the Dumpster. Now bits of chicken and lumpy white rice had found a home in his dark hair. At least he hoped it was white rice. No rats, thankfully, though he had stumbled upon one frightened brown mouse. After which, Xander had insisted to Cordelia that he did not, in fact, scream like a girl. Hey, the mouse could have had rabies for all he'd known.

"Nothing," Xander said. Nothing that would indicate

the presence of Willow or Troy. Everything else one could reasonably expect to find in a well-stocked Dumpster had found its way into his hair, shirt, trouser pockets, socks and shoes. If anything, he was starting to feel a real and abiding empathy for the life of a garbage dump rat. He reached out a brown-stained hand toward Cordelia. "Help me out."

"Oh, no," she said, shaking her head as she backed away. "Not till after you've bathed—at least several hundred times."

Oz stepped up, offered his hand and pulled Xander out of the muck. "Thanks, man," Oz said, indicating the state of Xander's skin and clothes.

After seeing the grim expression on Oz's face, Xander felt as if Dumpster diving was the least he could do to help. Xander and Willow had been friends, well, forever, it seemed. There was nothing he wouldn't do if it meant getting Will out of a jam. But she and Oz had something special and he knew Oz was hurting big time. "No problem, Oz," Xander said, and flicked a few grains of white rice out of his ear. "Just wish I could have found something useful in there."

"I know," Oz said, downcast. His flashlight beam shone on the side of the brown Dumpster, revealing a dark, splotchy stain.

They were standing in early predawn light that made the street lamps appear even fainter, but Xander noticed a distinct red hue to the stain and he doubted it was ketchup. He crouched beside the Dumpster and, despite his grime covered hands, was afraid to touch the wetness, afraid to confirm what he knew it must be. Remarkably, he caught a whiff of Cordelia's perfume as she stepped up beside him—remarkable because it was only in contrast to her scent that he realized how truly awful he smelled.

"Look," Cordelia said softly, pointing down beside him.

Xander nodded, dislodging a few more kernels of rice. "I know," he said. "Looks like blood."

Oz crouched and shone the light on the red stain.

"No," Cordelia said and picked up a piece of cloth which had been pinned against one of the Dumpster's wheels. "This," she said, showing it to them.

"A clothing label?" Xander said, confused.

"Duh—are you guys blind?" Cordelia asked. "It's Versace."

Oz frowned.

"Hello," she said. "Was no one paying attention? Troy was wearing Versace last night."

Buffy and Angel had just returned from another circuit of the Bronze. She examined the piece of cloth Cordelia held pinched between her fingernails, shining her own flashlight on the label, and realized the significance. "They—it—whatever got Troy," she said, glancing at Angel, who only nodded.

"I really hate this town," Cordelia said. "All the great guys get eaten by demons!"

"Oh, no—oh, no!" Xander shouted, pointing at the ground. "Guys, look! The rice—the rice is moving!" He yelled and ran, flicking his fingers through his hair and shuddering. "Oh, God—God! Beyond gross!"

Cordelia looked down to where Xander had pointed. "Is that—?"

Angel nodded. "Maggots."

Cordelia's hand went to her mouth. "Oh, I'm gonna be sick!"

"Aim for the Dumpster," Angel said.

Buffy walked over to where Oz had retreated, now almost oblivious to his surroundings. She put an arm around him. "We'll find her, Oz. I promise."

"Willow's alive," Oz said softly. "Bet on it."

Willow was alive, but she ached all over.

Vyxn had kept her tied up and gagged during the third set of their show, hunched over in a closet in their dressing room. On the other side of the closet, in a large sack, they had dumped what was left of Troy. And there hadn't been all that much after their set break meal. Despite their ravenous appetite for human flesh, they had been careful to remove all evidence of their attack outside the Bronze. Willow had not been hopeful that her friends would find her any time soon.

She still was not hopeful, especially since she had no idea where she was. They had put her in another foul-smelling sack and dumped her in the back of their van for the trip back to their hideout—lair?

A collar had been fastened around her neck and chained to a long board—with other, matching hooks—mounted to the wall of her room, where she sat and waited alone. The two windows on one side of the room were covered with old plywood. Early morning light streamed through narrow cracks, illuminating a cascade of dust motes. The walls were painted a sickly shade of green and, in several spots, plaster and lath showed through holes in the drywall.

She could hear the four of them, talking and laughing, almost as if they were human, which couldn't be further from the truth. Willow was no longer gagged but there was no use screaming. Lupa had told her the abandoned house was too isolated for screaming to do her any good. Nash had pretended to scream for help, just to show how hopeless it was. The others had laughed and left Willow alone for a while.

Now the door opened again as Carnie, the redheaded bassist, stepped inside, munching on what could probably be the remains of a human forearm. Beyond her, Willow could see Lupa, Rave and Nash at an old wooden table, busy with their own pounds of flesh. "Leftovers," Carnie said. "Want a bite?"

"No thanks, I already vomited."

Carnie laughed. "If you're gonna be one of us, you really have to get over this aversion to raw human flesh."

"That's really not a problem since, actually, I would really prefer not to be one of you."

Carnie chuckled and shrugged. "You're either one of us," she said and, by way of demonstrating, reverted to her mottled green, jagged-toothy self. "Or"—she waved the hunk of forearm in a slow arc—"you're one of them. Your call."

CHAPTER 9

"**O**kay, Giles," Buffy said beside Giles's hospital bed. "Here are the Watchers' journals and the other musty books you requested." She placed the old, leather-bound tomes on the movable hospital tray, where they were bound to unsettle the nurses.

"Thank you, Buffy."

"Looks like the Watchers Council bestsellers list or something."

"Certain volumes—the *Pergamum Codex*, the *Black Chronicles*, the *Writings of Dramius*, to name a few— have, over time, proven invaluable, yes," Giles said.

"And somehow not an Oprah pick in the bunch."

"You were able to complete the uninvite ritual successfully?" Giles asked.

Buffy gave a brisk nod. "Dotted my T's and crossed

my I's. Took over right where you left off when you were so rudely interrupted," she said. "Or was that the other way around?" The smile on her face faded as if it had been an illusion all along. She pulled up a chair and sat close to her Watcher. "Okay, Giles, spill. My mom said you called to tell me you were in the hospital but okay." Her gaze swept across the cast on his arm, the bandage on his forehead. "You don't look 'okay.' "

"Nothing too serious," Giles said. "Concussion, fractured wrist, skull lacerations. Humbling, but hardly life-threatening. Now tell me. Have you been able to locate Willow?"

Buffy pushed herself out of the hospital chair and walked to the window, staring down between the gaps in the vertical blinds at the orderly rows of parked cars. *I should be doing something—anything—if I only knew where to start.* Willow was her best friend and all Buffy could say was, "No."

"Still nothing to indicate she disappeared from the Bronze? Or Troy?"

"We think Troy may have run into the flesh-eaters, the ghouls or whatever they are," Buffy said. "After he left the Bronze. Cordelia identified a piece of clothing and there was some blood. But we can't be sure if Willow was there or—"

"I know," Giles said. "If nothing else, the lack of physical evidence gives us reason for hope that she's okay."

Buffy nodded, returning to his bedside. "Xander and Oz promised to catch a few hours sleep. But they're probably out searching again by now."

"You'll be missed at school. Your mother?"

"Called in to cover for me. But that probably won't stop Principal Snyder from taking his evil little chart to my commando counselor to show her what a horribly undedicated student I am."

"Buffy, you mustn't neglect your studies," Giles said. "Or your sleep. You need to prepare yourself for the challenges ahead. Otherwise you will be of no use to Willow or yourself. With our resources spread thin, we must approach this intelligently and efficiently." Giles flipped through one of the larger tomes, frowned, closed it and selected another. He jabbed at a page with his good index finger. "There is mention of flesh-eating ghouls here," he said. "As I said before, creatures out of Arabic folklore." He skimmed the passage, culling the salient facts. "Ghouls were female desert demons who lured travelers—we can assume men—into their clutches and devoured them."

"No deserts in Sunnydale," Buffy said. She tapped her head. "See—got that whole intelligence thing working now."

"But we do have a Hellmouth."

"Okay, but this Solitaire guy doesn't fit the pattern," Buffy said. "First off, he's a guy. Second, if he was a ghoul, you would have been an entrée."

"No, I believe Solitaire is a loner," Giles said. "As evidenced by his name and notwithstanding his playing-card affectation. I'm afraid Solitaire is nothing more than a vampire, a very powerful vampire."

"A vampire who slaps on some SPF 10,000 before a morning stroll?"

Giles frowned. "There is that—er, anomaly. We can't discount the possibility that he possesses a magical ring or an amulet that protects him from the rays of the sun. Make a note. You'll want to remove that if you encounter him in daylight."

"Or I could just stake him."

"Quite right," Giles conceded. "I do recall mention of a vampire named Solitaire in a Watchers' journal. But the entry dates back three or four hundred years." He pushed aside the larger books and started flipping through the assorted Watchers' journals. He shook his head, disappointed he couldn't immediately locate entries he had read years ago. "The subject of rumors and myth spread by the legions of undead who feared him. I suppose I've forgotten the specific entries since there's been no mention of him for hundreds of years."

"What did he say to you, Giles?"

"He basically threatened your life," Giles said.

"That's original."

"He was, however, quite impressed with your reputation," Giles said.

"Color me flattered."

"This is quite serious, Buffy," Giles said. "He seemed particularly impressed with the way you handled the Order of Taraka. Apparently, he now considers you a challenge worthy of him."

"Sounds like a Wild West gunfighter," Buffy said.

"The parallel is not without merit," Giles said.

"And that biker—Warhammer—was what? A warm-up act?" Buffy guessed.

"The other bikers who were killed simply got in the way. Solitaire challenged Warhammer directly, the others he offered a chance to escape. Your mother and I are probably alive simply because we are beneath his notice."

"If he wants me," Buffy said. "Why not come directly to me?"

"He's circling you, sizing you up, looking for weaknesses," Giles said. "If he savors the duel, it is reasonable to assume he savors the anticipation of the duel as well. He's engaging in a psychological battle before the physical battle."

"What he's doing is getting me really angry."

"He will look for the advantage before attacking. If he truly is immune to the rays of the sun, you must be on your guard all the time, day and night."

Willow could no longer deny she was hungry. Whenever her stomach growled, she thought about what had happened to Troy and instantly lost her appetite. But the image was losing its power over her building hunger. Sleep helped pass the time, but the hardwood floor was uncomfortable and she woke every fifteen minutes or so with stiff and achy limbs. So she had fatigue to add to her list of grievances.

To keep herself occupied while awake, she examined the iron collar they had put on her neck. It felt old, handmade, but sturdy. The padlock also had an Old World, pre-industrial–age quality to it. However, the chain holding her to the ring board was made of identical, machine-stamped, stainless-steel links. She tried unscrewing the ring from the board but it was impossible without leverage. The board was securely mounted to the wall and— she guessed from the even horizontal spacing of the nails—into the beams of the house. Of course, at least one member of Vyxn had stayed in the house since they had locked her in the room, so she had been careful not to make too much noise.

She turned away from the wall as she heard the door open.

Carnie again, but this time with Lupa, the ghoul leader. They took positions on either side of her, both wearing their human disguises. Beyond them, sitting at a table bathed in the wan light of a hanging oil lantern, Willow could see Rave and Nash. Both were in their natural ghoul form, bristling with jagged teeth and sharp claws, the better to strip meat off the bones, as they talked in low tones. The slaughterhouse stench made Willow's stomach turn, though she couldn't help but be relieved when Lupa swung the door shut which, if nothing else, blocked the revolting scene in the other room.

"Any preference for take-out?" Carnie asked. "Thai? Mexican? Chinese?"

"I'm not hungry," Willow lied. "Thank you very much."

"You will be," Lupa assured her.

"What exactly do you want from me?"

Lupa crouched beside her. "We just want you to join our little club. All it takes is a . . . well, let's call it an *initiation*."

"Initiation?" Willow really didn't want to hear any more, nor did she believe she could get these ghouls to see the error of their ways, but the more she learned, the better her chances of figuring a way out of her predicament. And right now she could use an edge. *Any edge.*

"It's simple, really," Lupa told her. "All you have to do is consume the living flesh of your closest friend."

"About a quarter-pound should do it," Carnie added.

"What if, instead, I just make a really mean crank call?" Willow asked.

Lupa slapped her across the face, just hard enough to stun her. "Tell us about Buffy."

"Buffy—who?" Willow pressed her hand to her burning cheek. "She's not my—we've only seen—passed in the halls once or twice. I don't even think I know her last name. Why do you ask?"

"Nice try," Lupa said. She stood up. "We don't want to get ugly, and torture is such an *ugly* word. But we won't go there . . . yet. Right now, we have to get ready for our show. So, think about it. You still have time. Time to get good and hungry."

They left her alone, closing the door behind them. In the outer room, they talked softly among themselves but their voices were too faint to hear. It was much darker now. As the light faded, so too did her hope.

"Well?" Rave asked when Carnie and Lupa rejoined her and Nash at the table, in the center of which was a large bowl filled with gleaming, discarded bones.

"Not so loud," Lupa cautioned as she sat at the head of the table. "She's still the brave little soldier."

Nash gnawed patiently on a dismembered hand, snapping off finger joints after she'd picked them clean, then tossing them into the overflowing bowl. She nodded her head toward the closed door with a look of disgust. "No way is that one ghoul material, I say."

"It doesn't matter," Rave said, finishing a long strip of thigh meat.

"What?" Nash asked.

"You're forgetting," Lupa explained. "The ceremony doesn't have to be voluntary. After the transformation it won't matter anymore. She'll be one of us, part of the troupe."

Nash licked her clawed fingers. "The glam one," she said. "The brunette with the hot temper. She's the better choice, is what I think."

"This one fell into our claws," Lupa said. "She may not be the Slayer, but she doesn't let her fear consume her. There's a strength within her. I can sense it."

"Nothing but trouble, I say," Nash replied.

"Well, we need to increase our number," Lupa continued. "We can use a new keyboard player. So it might as well be her. Besides, if she causes too much trouble, we can always kill her later. For now, I need her alive."

Carnie grinned. "Ah . . . Slayer bait."

"You really think the Slayer will come for her?" Rave asked.

"We've seen the Slayer's circle of friends," Lupa said. "Imagine each and every one of them as a chink in her armor. They will lead her to us and she will sacrifice herself for them."

Xander felt as exhausted as Oz looked. They had been searching Sunnydale for most of the day and well into the evening for any sign of Willow. For what it was worth, Willow's parents had reported her disappearance to the police. Sunnydale's finest had, of course, mentioned a twenty-four-hour waiting period even though they understood that, yes, it was completely out of character for Willow Rosenberg to just drop out of sight. Eventually they would go through the motions, put out an APB—if they even did that sort of thing for missing persons—hand out flyers and check bus terminals. Officially, they'd probably chalk her up as a runaway teen. Xander wondered if the police would ever admit to themselves, deep down, that Willow had probably run afoul of the unexplained phenomena that plagued Sunnydale. More likely, however, they had convinced themselves—for their own peace of mind—that Sunnydale's history of death, destruction and disappearances was, really, not all that uncommon.

Oz and Xander had checked all the usual haunts and all the places where the various Hellmouth denizens had, at one time or another, caused problems. They had even driven to the UC Sunnydale campus in Oz's van and shown Willow's picture around.

Now Xander leaned against a tree in Weatherly Park and massaged his feet through his sneakers. "My blisters have spawned little blisters of their own."

Oz stood there with his hands stuffed in his pockets and just shook his head. "Go home. Get some rest."

"What about you?"

"I'm okay. I'm good."

"No offense, Oz," Xander said. "But you look like hell."

"I'll grab a coffee."

"At this point, you'd have to inject the java right in a vein," Xander said. "Besides, remember what Giles said. We who fit the young-men-who-get-eaten profile should not be out wandering alone at night. We won't do Willow much good in a stew pot."

"Any suggestions?"

"We go home. Grab a couple hours shut-eye. Start all over again."

"I don't know—"

"Look, Buffy and Angel are out by now, looking for Willow," Xander said. "The Slayerette flag will be flying at all times."

Oz sighed, giving in to the exhaustion. "Okay." They started toward Oz's van, which was at the far end of the park. "But just a few hours."

"What's the deal on this Solitaire guy? Should I be worried?" Buffy asked Angel. Since she'd told him about Solitaire's contact with her mother and Giles, Angel had been quiet and thoughtful. The longer he remained quiet on the subject, the more nervous she became.

They were patrolling Sunnydale Cemetery, on the assumption that whoever or whatever had dropped Robert John Wallace's femur and high school ring there might return to the scene of the disposal. Afterward, she and Angel planned to revisit Weatherly Park, specifically the site of the bone pit. If the flesh-eaters were responsible for Willow's disappearance and Buffy managed to get her hands on them, she had no doubt she could convince them to take her to Willow.

"I've been trying to remember what I've heard about him," Angel said.

"So you never ran into him yourself?"

Angel shook his head. "A vampire called Solitaire

roamed across Europe. He traveled alone, seeking and killing powerful vampires. Many vampires feared this obsession of his. But that period predates me by over a hundred years. All I've heard are the legends—rumors really."

"Killing vampires, huh?" Buffy said. "Surprised nobody reported him to the Slayer union? That's our job."

"He challenged them to duels. One on one," Angel said. "I really can't recall anyone talking about him for over a century. Guess I assumed he'd finally met his match, picked the wrong fight."

"Maybe this is a different bad guy," Buffy said.

Again, Angel shook his head. "It's either him or somebody imitating him. Since we're talking about a vampire here, I tend to believe the former. Challenging Warhammer to a duel certainly fits his pattern."

"Warhammer, not a vampire," Buffy reminded him.

Angel shrugged. "Say he's looking for a new thrill. Maybe he became bored dueling vampires, which would account for his dropping off the underworld radar. Warhammer was the toughest fighter in the biker gang. Solitaire sought him out. Probably considered it a light workout, a sparring match." Buffy stopped. Angel turned to her. "What?"

"I just realized it's been too quiet lately," she said meaningfully.

Angel caught her meaning. "Skull John."

"Even money Solitaire took him out."

"He certainly would have drawn Solitaire's attention. And you—" Angel said, concerned. "From what he told

Giles, your reputation apparently precedes you. You're the main event."

"So . . . while I'm trying to find Willow, this Solitaire guy is lining me up in his crosshairs."

"No, it's personal with this guy," Angel said. "He won't strike from a distance. He'll want you to see it coming."

"Great, maybe he'll send an RSVP," Buffy said and sighed. "Regrets only."

"He'll bring it to you," Angel said. "But you're not alone. You know that."

Buffy kissed him lightly on the lips. "Ah, my guardian Angel."

Oz might have caught a few winks in between all the tossing and turning. Thoughts of Willow in jeopardy had fended off his attempts to sleep, to get some rest. He'd forced himself to stay in bed, restless, for a couple hours. Finally, he couldn't wait around any longer. He'd climbed into his van and had driven across town with no particular destination in mind. Just searching, endlessly searching with no clue where to go next, but at least he was doing something. Then even that wasn't enough. He pulled over to the curb, outside the entrance to Weatherly Park, where he and Xander had searched just hours ago. The location brought home the futility of the search. *This is nuts!*

He stepped out of the van, slammed the door, and soon found himself pacing on the sidewalk, trying to think of something he hadn't done, someplace he hadn't searched. With a frustrated sigh, he sat on a bench next to a pay phone, elbows on his knees, hands pressed against the sides of his head.

He breathed deeply, several times, trying to get control of himself.

That's when he realized something else had been bothering him. And it only took a moment to put a name to it. *Vyxn.* The band should be the last thing on his mind. Yet, there it was, like an itch under his skin he couldn't quite scratch. He was missing their show. Their last set would almost be over by now . . . and that was driving him crazy. *Withdrawal* was a term that came to mind. Of course, Cordelia would probably chalk it up to raging male hormones.

To take his mind off of Lupa and the rest of Vyxn, Oz decided to check in with Buffy, see if she'd found any clues to Willow's whereabouts, even though he was sure she would have contacted him with any new information. Regardless, it was something to take his mind off of Vyxn. Then he'd call Xander and arrange to pick him up at his house to renew their search.

Oz put change into the pay phone slot and dialed Buffy's number, only to have her mother answer. He was about to leave a message with her when she stopped him midsentence. "Oh—wait, I think that's her now."

A moment later, Buffy picked up the phone. "Oz, I'm so sorry. We haven't been able to find anything new. This is driving me crazy, so I can only imagine how you must feel. Have you and Xander had any luck?"

"Nothing."

"Have you guys managed any sleep?"

"Does tossing and turning count?"

"Not as much as it should, unfortunately," Buffy said.

"Giles keeps reminding me to keep up my strength. That goes for you guys, too."

"Buffy," Oz said. "Thanks."

"We'll find her, Oz," Buffy said. "Willow is nothing if not resourceful and not just because of that whole Wicca power thing."

"I know."

Before he could hang up, Buffy said, "Giles dug up a reference in Arabic folklore about desert dwelling flesh-eaters. It describes ghouls as female desert demons with the ability to lure men into their clutches and, apparently, right onto the buffet table. Stay close to Xander. Don't go out alone."

Good advice. As soon as I pick up Xander, I won't be alone anymore. "How is Giles?"

"Slightly broken," Buffy said. "They want to keep him overnight for observation. Solitaire could have done major damage, but he only wanted to rough up Giles to rattle me. I told Giles nobody messes with my Watcher."

"Be careful, Buffy."

"You too, Oz."

After Oz hung up the phone, he called Xander's house, only to discover that Xander had left home over an hour ago with a vague reference to the Bronze. Mention of the Bronze brought the itch back. Since Xander had already gone to the Bronze, Oz would have to drive there to pick him up. He might even catch the last song or two. Maybe get that itch out of his skin. It was a weak rationalization, but he didn't have much choice anyway.

Halfway to the Bronze, he caught himself speeding, clutching the steering wheel with white-knuckled intensity. He realized he was desperate to see Vyxn before their show ended. And that brought back Buffy's words ... *ghouls, female desert demons with the ability to lure men into their clutches.*

The Bronze.

Troy had been attacked outside the Bronze.

Willow had likely been on her way to the Bronze to meet Oz when she disappeared.

Moreover, Xander—even though he had agreed to wait for Oz to pick him up at home—had gone to the Bronze. *Had been lured there?*

Oz no longer fought the unnatural urge to see Vyxn. He wanted to see them as soon as possible. They would lead him to Willow.

The Bronze.

CHAPTER 10

Xander had no idea why he'd returned to the Bronze.
He was still exhausted after little more than an hour of
sleep. All he remembered was sitting up in bed with the
disturbing realization that he was missing the show. He
knew if he hurried, he could catch the last set and then
meet up with Oz afterward. That wasn't being disloyal to
Willow, was it? If it seemed irrational, even to him, he
decided it was due to sleep deprivation. *Simpler to just
give in to the urge . . .*

When the last song ended, Lupa addressed the
crowd, which was predominantly male. "Thanks, guys,
you're great! Come see our final show, tomorrow. Now
go home . . . and you'll see us in your dreams!" She
laughed and the crowd roared, including Xander.

Xander felt even more exhausted. What little energy

he'd had, had fled with the last notes of the encore. Nevertheless, he found himself rising from his chair when he caught a look from Lupa. She held up her index finger and mouthed a single word: *Wait*.

The rest of the band filed backstage. Lupa stepped down off the stage and sat opposite him at the small table. She placed the wireless microphone on the table. "Well?" she asked.

"Killer show."

"Definitely," Lupa said with a wry smile.

Again, Xander was struck by her lack of perspiration. The hot stage lights alone should raise a sheen of sweat, he thought. "It borders on boggling that I've never heard of Vyxn before."

"We've been around . . . *forever*," she said with another mysterious grin. "At least it seems that way. So, what took you so long?" Xander arched his eyebrows in question. "You came in during our last set."

"Ah, I was out looking . . ." Xander sighed and turned away as a wave of guilt swept over him. "Nothing."

She whispered his name, took his chin in her hand and turned his face toward hers. "Tell me what's wrong, Xander." Her voice was strangely hypnotic, compelling.

"I—I was worried about a missing friend," he said. "I should be out looking for her, not sitting here with you. No offense."

"None taken," Lupa said. "Who is this missing friend?"

"Uh—Willow," Xander said. He wanted to tell her all about it, but resisted the . . . compulsion.

"You and Willow are close?"

"We're best buds from way back."

"You don't say," Lupa said. "Listen, I'd like to do something to cheer you up."

"Probably not possible at the moment."

"Come back to the dressing room," she said. "For autographs. I'll even see if I can dig up a demo tape."

"I—I really shouldn't," Xander said, though the idea was mighty tempting.

"Come on," she said. "Just take a minute or two. Besides, I think Carnie has a crush on you. Hey, we could even ride you around in our van, look for Willow. She'll be impressed when she sees you have the entire band out looking for her. What do you say?" Lupa noticed a couple high school–aged guys lingering near the table, eavesdropping and clearly envious of Xander's position. She glared at them. Another time they would be tempting morsels, but right now they were an annoyance. *"Go home,* I told you." They mumbled something apologetic and shuffled off, like good little sheep. "What's it gonna be, Xander?"

It was almost as if she knew he couldn't refuse her offer. *Just a minute or two,* he thought, rationalizing. *Just a minute or two couldn't hurt.* "Lead the way," Xander said, finally giving in, a giddy smile on his face.

None of the others seemed surprised to see him enter their dressing room. Carnie winked and said, "Hi, Xander."

Xander noticed all the band posters that had been taped up on the walls over the years, each signed by the members of the respective bands. He even saw a Dingoes poster with "OZ" scrawled on it. *The inner sanctum.*

"You'll never guess who his *best* friend is," Lupa said to them as she closed the door.

Carnie raised her hand and said, "Who is Willow, Alex?"

"Wow," Xander said. "How did you—?"

He turned around to face Lupa, but in her place was a green-skinned creature with rows of sharp teeth holding the wireless microphone in a clawed hand. Xander realized he'd found the ghouls . . . or they'd found him.

"Simple," the ghoul Lupa said. "Willow's almost like a sister to us."

She swung the wireless mike like a club.

Oz had missed the entire show. He knew because a bunch of high school guys were streaming out of the Bronze as he pulled up. They looked tired and dejected. An ache filled the pit of his stomach. He really needed to hear them perform again. He'd lost his chance for that, so he tried to focus on his other reason for rushing to the Bronze. Xander. He'd come for Xander . . . and to find out if Vyxn was somehow responsible for Willow's disappearance.

Somebody familiar from school was coming out of the Bronze. Oz edged through the crowd and called out. "Hey, Jake. Seen Xander lately?"

"You know it," he said. "Lucky jerk."

"What?"

"Vyxn, well, the singer, Lupa, invited him backstage." Jake shook his head in disbelief. "First he hooks up with Cordelia Chase. Now this. Can you believe his luck?"

Unfortunately, Oz had the sinking feeling Xander's

luck had taken a decided turn for the worse. "Thanks, man." Oz worked his way against the tide, through the last stragglers to find his way into the Bronze. Almost every table was empty. Xander was nowhere around.

Oz knew his way backstage. The corridor was dark, but navigable. He found their dressing room. Black marker on a strip of masking tape spelled out VYXN. He listened at the door, heard nothing, tried the handle and opened the door.

The room was empty.

I'm too late.

"At least we know he was here, seen talking to the band before he disappeared," Buffy said. She and Angel had joined Oz, but the three of them combined had turned up little additional information in the search for Xander. "What did the Bronze's manager say again?" Buffy asked Oz for about the third time since she'd arrived with Angel. "No mailing address?"

Oz shook his head. "Rust-colored van. Tinted windows."

"Not much to go on," Angel said.

"How did he contact them?" Buffy asked.

"They contacted him," Oz said. "Performed a song."

Buffy shook her head. "And he hired them on the spot. Why am I not surprised?"

They had driven around for over an hour, in a widening radius, looking for that van but without success. Finally they had returned to the scene of the disappearance, the Bronze.

Buffy sighed. "I should have seen this coming."

"How could you?" Oz asked.

"I knew there was something strange about Vyxn," Buffy said. "I just chalked it up to—"

"Raging male hormones?" Oz asked wryly.

"Unfortunately," Buffy said.

"Hiding in plain sight," Angel said.

"What?"

"Vyxn," he said. "They were clever. Right out in the open. Posters and special engagements, skimpy outfits . . . all so no one would suspect anything but the obvious attraction."

"I'm worried about Xander," Buffy said. "Even more so than Willow. He fits the profile for a ghoulish Happy Meal. Maybe we should call Giles. See if he's found anything that might help us locate them."

"Worth a try," Oz said.

A call to the hospital revealed that Giles had checked himself out against medical advice. Buffy tried her mother next, figuring Giles might have left a message for her there. After hanging up the pay phone, she turned to the others. "Giles called. He's back at his place now."

"Let's go," Oz said.

"Giles, shouldn't you still be under a doctor's care?"

"My stay in hospital was purely precautionary," Giles said. "Besides, I had exhausted the reference volumes and journals you'd brought me, so I checked myself out. And, quite frankly, there were too many . . . distractions at the hospital for me to continue productive research."

"Distractions?" Buffy asked.

"Well, there was the matter of the old nurse who actually screamed when she glimpsed the color illustration of the Slighohr demon feeding off the entrails of marooned sailors."

"Nurses generally aren't the squeamish sort," Oz said.

"It was a rather realistic illustration."

Giles sipped from a cup of Earl Grey tea, mindful of his arm in a cast, with a bandage around his forehead. Each time he needed to turn the pages of the book that currently held his interest, he had to place the cup down on the table first. Watching him, Buffy couldn't help but feel as if she were letting down everyone who was close to her. Because she was the Slayer, she'd placed her mother at risk, Willow had disappeared right out from under her, then Giles had taken a beating just to get a rise out of her and now Xander had been kidnapped by flesh-eating ghouls. She had never felt so helpless. To take her mind off the sudden, crushing wave of guilt, Buffy turned her attention to business, Slayer business. "Tell me more about these desert ghouls," she said. "Any reason why they would decide to form a rock band?"

"Creatures who endure centuries or even millennia preying on humankind for sustenance must adapt to human society or become extinct."

"I'm good with Plan B," Oz said.

"Historically, these Arabic ghouls preyed on isolated travelers, using a siren's song, as it were, to lure men to their doom," Giles said. "Yet as the world population has grown, areas of isolation have decreased. It would appear that these ghouls have reinvented themselves in order to lure their prey. Forced into the light of day and into social surroundings, they have adapted their methods in a manner likely to lure their chosen prey."

"A sexy girl band to attract male groupies," Buffy said.

"It would appear so," Giles said. "Yes."

"So they can hide their true appearance just like—" Her gaze found Angel.

"Vampires," he finished.

"So what do we do now?"

Giles pushed his glasses up the bridge of his nose. "The band is scheduled to perform one more night, correct?" Oz nodded. "Then, regardless of how agonizing it is, we must wait till after their performance tomorrow night and follow them back to their lair."

"Why wait?" Buffy said. "I say we crash the party."

"What if you kill them all? Or one should happen to escape and return to their lair?"

Buffy frowned. "Do we really have any other options?"

"Since you were unable to find any evidence that Vyxn, er, disposed of Xander on the premises, we must hope that they are keeping him alive, somewhere, in a sort of larder."

"What guarantee do we have that they'll keep him alive?"

"None, I'm afraid," Giles admitted. "But we know they prefer raw flesh. If they don't kill him before their show, he will still be alive after, at least for a while. Safer to follow them than to attempt to capture them without knowing the location of the lair."

Buffy nodded. "It's a plan."

Angel glanced at the clock, then looked to Buffy. "I should get back."

Before they left, Giles caught Oz's arm with his good hand. "Oz, it is quite possible that they are holding Willow alive with Xander. You mustn't give up hope."

Oz nodded slightly and said, "Thanks."

As Giles's door opened, Solitaire backed into the shadows and waited. The Slayer was accompanied by her pet vampire—the one she called Angel—and by another young man who was not altogether human, if Solitaire was any judge. But the other was of little concern to him now. It would soon be dawn and the pet vampire would be in a hurry to hide from the sun. Solitaire smiled. Angel would soon have more to worry about than the burning rays of the sun.

From the sheer boredom of her confinement, Willow had dozed occasionally and uncomfortably on the hardwood floor. Sometimes she would prop her back against the wall, but that position never lasted. She had just dozed off again when she heard the sound of a struggle coming from the outer room. With the door to her room closed, she couldn't see who was fighting out there. Although her first thought was that someone had come to rescue her, she recognized the possibility that ghouls could have enemies just as dangerous to humans as they were. Especially to humans who were helpless and conveniently chained to a wall. "Who . . . who is it?" she called tentatively.

She sat up straighter, pressing her back to the wall, her chain rattling slightly. A moment later the door was kicked in, shattering the frame near the doorknob. The white-haired Rave and the redheaded Carnie each held an arm of their captive, a young guy who struggled fiercely. Nash squeezed by them and slipped a chain through a wall ring next to Willow's, while Rave and Carnie dragged the guy into the room. Though Willow couldn't see his face in the dim light, there was something familiar about his build.

Lupa, the leader of the ghouls, stepped in last. She stood in front of the guy and shouted, "Enough!" She punched him hard in the gut to punctuate her command. As he doubled over in pain, gasping for air, she slapped an old iron collar around his neck. Nash lined up the chain and slipped the post of a large padlock through the chain and the ring built into the collar. It snapped shut with an eerie finality.

"Manacles," Lupa said to Nash. The ghoul with the spiked collar nodded, left the room and returned with a pair of centuries-old manacles, two big cuffs connected by less than a foot of chain. Carnie and Rave pulled his arms back and held them pinned while Nash locked the cuffs with a long key on an old-fashioned jailer's key ring.

As they stepped away, the guy fell on his side, still coughing and sputtering from the hard punch Lupa had landed. Finally, Willow saw his face. "Xander?" she whispered. Catching herself, she cleared her throat and said, "I . . . I mean, who is he?"

Xander struggled into a sitting position. "Will? Is that you?"

Still struggling to come to grips with his imprisonment, Xander had only regained consciousness as Rave and Carnie had carried him out of the Vyxn van toward their dilapidated house. As they had maneuvered him through the front door, he was remembering what Lupa looked like when she wasn't wearing her human disguise. That's when he had started thrashing, but to no avail. All too soon he had been beaten and chained. The sole bright spot had been finding Willow alive. Yet, for some reason, she was pretending not to know him. "Will? What's up?"

She refused to look at him. "Sorry. Not knowing you."

By the meager light of an oil lantern hanging in the outer room, Xander took in their surroundings, hoping to notice some clue to Willow's odd behavior. They were in a rectangular room, fourteen feet long, maybe ten feet wide and chained to the wall opposite the door, no more than four feet apart from each other. The only light source was a hanging oil lantern in the other room, turned down low. To their right was a double window frame, covered with strips of plywood where the glass should have been. Where the sections met were narrow gaps which would probably allow thin shafts of sunlight to stream through during the day, but night, especially this close to the full moon, provided relatively no ambient light. The walls had been painted an unpleasant shade of green some time ago, with lighter square sections marking the former positions of pictures or mirrors. Down along the baseboard were holes in the wall where power outlets or phone jacks had been. Overhead was a single light fixture, missing a bulb.

Most troubling to Xander was the stench wafting in from the outer room. Years ago he'd found a dead field mouse behind his parents' sofa a couple days after it had died. Finding the mouse hadn't been a problem. The strong smell of decay had led him right to it. What he smelled in the ghoul's house was a thousand times worse. Knowing the probable source of that foul odor was making him gag.

Lupa stood before Willow and him, Rave and Carnie flanking her, while Nash stayed in back leaning against the doorframe. "He's says you two are close," Lupa said to Willow.

"No—not at all," Willow said quickly. "He's a complete stranger. We've never met."

"That's strange," Lupa replied. "Because he described you two as 'best buds.'"

Xander looked back and forth between them. "What's going on, Will? Instructions enclosed or what?"

"It's simple," Willow whispered urgently. "You don't know me."

"What? I've known you practically my whole life, we—"

"Sounds like we have our man," Carnie said.

"What have you done to Willow?" Xander yelled. "What's going on!"

"Oh, we just needed to find Willow's best friend for a little ceremony we will perform during the new moon which, I might add, just happens to be tomorrow night."

Even though Xander had been knocked around quite a bit, he had the distinct impression he'd just shown his hangman the proper way to tie a noose. "I'm not real big on ceremonies."

Willow said, "Trust me, Xander, you don't want to know."

"It's kind of a blah-blah-blah, boring old bloodletting ceremony, right up until the end," Carnie explained. "But that's the exciting part. You see, right at the end, Willow here gets to eat the living flesh of her best friend and become a sister ghoul."

Xander's eyes had progressively widened. "Willow? Become one of the Spice Ghouls? Never! Right, Will?"

Willow was quiet, head down, chin against her chest.

"Willow? Mind backing me up here? Remember that whole 'human beings do not eat their own kind' thing we joke about in the cafeteria on Sloppy Joe Tuesdays?"

Willow looked up at the ghouls, not Xander. "I won't do it."

Lupa crouched down in front of her. "Don't be so sure about that, little girl. When the alternatives are so much worse, you will do whatever we tell you."

Willow spat in her face. Lupa only blinked. "It's just a matter of time. Less than twenty-four hours, actually."

Xander hurled himself at Lupa. If he'd had enough slack in the chain or if his hands hadn't been manacled behind his back, he might have reached her, done some damage. Instead, straining against his chain, he slipped and fell sideways. Lupa walked over to him and kicked him hard in the stomach.

"You do want the whole twenty-four hours, don't you?" Lupa said. While he retched and gasped for air, a line of spittle stretching from his mouth to the floor, she crouched down beside him and spoke in a caressing whisper. "Listen to me, Xander. *There's no hope.*" And for a brief moment, he believed her, utterly, as if the statement bore the weight of his own, real desolation. He trembled uncontrollably in the wake of icy despair. "That's better," Lupa commented, standing again.

"We have two of them now," Rave remarked. "Do you think the Slayer will show?"

"Oh, she'll show," Lupa said. "I'll make sure of that. Even if we have to leave a trail of breadcrumbs."

"What do you want with Buffy?" Willow asked Lupa. It was much too late to pretend she didn't know her friends.

"What do I want with the Slayer?" Lupa's skin turned its natural, mottled green. She bared her uneven rows of fangs and slowly made a clawed fist, as if squeezing something she held in her hand. "Oh, just a few bites of her still beating heart should do it. But that's a ceremony of a different color altogether."

Carnie laughed wickedly. "Still, a two-for-one would be kinda special."

Nash chuckled. "A Slayer special, I say."

Xander was curled up on the floor, still in too much pain to speak as the ghouls left the room. They pulled the door closed, but the busted doorframe no longer held it secure. As it creaked open, a pale shaft of light widened across the floor, keeping them from total darkness. He could hear them laughing out there, even as he groaned.

Willow sidled over to Xander and saw, in the dim light, the lump on his forehead. "Xander—are you okay? Relatively speaking, that is."

"It—it freaked me out, what she said," Xander said. "Like that time on my bike and that car barely missed me. I couldn't stop shaking."

"It's gone now? The feeling, I mean."

Xander nodded, almost afraid to confirm it out loud.

"I'll live," he said. "At least up until the part where the ghouls kill me. That's me talking, by the way."

"I can tell the difference," Willow said with a brief nod. "Quite a mess we've gotten ourselves into."

He struggled to a sitting position, careful of his tender stomach and his cramped arms as he leaned back against the wall. "Next Slayerette meeting, you can bet I'm demanding hazard pay. Now answer a question for me."

"What?"

"What is that sound?"

"My stomach," Willow said, slightly embarrassed. "It's growling."

His eyes widened. "Growling?"

"I'm *really* hungry," she said.

"Hungry like 'I'll have a second piece of pie.' Right? Not hungry as in, 'Ooh, my best friend's lookin' kinda tasty tonight.' "

"I could probably eat the whole pie."

"Okay . . . 'cause, for a second there, you know, you had me worried. Now, let's see . . ." Xander twisted his arms behind his back to get a hand in his trouser pocket.

"What are you doing?"

"Well, if I'm not mistaken, there should be several ounces of chocolate goodness in my left front pocket."

"Xander, if you have chocolate in your pants I'll love you forever!"

Xander quirked an eyebrow. "Okay, not the strangest pick-up line I've heard, but—" He finally managed to tug a chocolate bar out of his pocket. He held it out to Willow between his index and middle fingers. "Might be a little mushy."

"I don't care." She ripped off the wrapper. After popping several squares into her mouth, she mumbled, "Oh—you probably want some too."

"No, no, enjoy," Xander said. "I had something earlier. Besides, the important thing here is to keep *your* belly full and non-grumbly."

Willow paused with only a square or two of chocolate left. "What are we gonna do, Xander? I'm worried."

"You're worried? I'm scheduled to be the chef's special tomorrow." Xander's tone was light, to put her at ease, but his false bravado was a thin veneer. He was more worried than he cared to admit.

"They can't make me eat you, Xander."

"They are supernatural fiends," Xander said. "We don't know what they can make either one of us do."

"We have to figure out a way to warn Buffy."

"Yeah, Will," Xander said grimly. "If we can't get out of these collars and chains, Buffy may be the only one who can help us out of this mess."

CHAPTER 11

*B*uffy couldn't help her friends or herself.

She felt utterly useless.

Sitting in her bed, back propped against a couple pillows, she stared at the telephone messages her mother had taped to her bedroom door, right at eye level, so Buffy would be sure to see them. She held them in her hand now. Both from Mrs. Burzak, whose not-so-secret identity was Commando Counselor. The first message expressed deep concern with Buffy's absence from her yellow and red zone classes, while the second reminded her that she had important exams tomorrow in two of those classes, yellow calculus and red history. Fail those classes and she would probably fail the year.

Problem was, *tomorrow* was already here, the exams

only several hours away. With Willow and then Xander disappearing, it had been hard to even think about studying. She was running out of time and options if she intended to help her friends or herself. Giles had kept insisting to Oz and her, "There's nothing you can do for Willow and Xander until *after* Vyxn's show. So rest and be ready." Her Watcher made sense, as usual. Still, she hated the waiting, if not quite as much as the aimless searching. The truly maddening had been replaced by the completely frustrating. *We know who the ghouls are now,* she thought, *and we have a plan.* Unfortunately, part of the plan was . . . waiting.

She heaved a sigh and pushed away a sloppy pile of notebooks filled with her own ballpoint hieroglyphics. Too restless to sleep, Buffy flipped through the mind-numbing pages of her textbooks. Her hopes of salvaging a high school diploma seemed an exercise in futility at this point. If she hadn't gleaned enough from her studies of the past several days . . . well, summer school was always an option.

By the time the birds had gotten fairly vocal about the possibilities of the new day, she had dozed off, textbooks strewn across her bed sheets. Even though her alarm that morning seemed unusually abrasive and unwelcome, she fought off a compelling urge to slap the snooze button.

She arrived at school and, specifically, the library much earlier than was her custom. Even Principal Snyder seemed surprised as he filled in his little clipboard chart. *Probably wished he could tag my ear and monitor my progress like a migratory bird.* Since he secretly wanted her to fail and ultimately face expulsion, she took satisfaction in knowing she had probably ruined his current mood, if not his entire day. Her own mood was tempered by the realization that her two big exams were only a couple hours away.

As she walked into the library, Giles looked up from an oversized and water-stained Watcher tome, its leather binding exhibiting extreme signs of distress. "Oh, Buffy, good, you're early. Before I forget—and I know you have a lot to be concerned about—Mrs. Burzak made me promise to remind you—"

"About my exams," Buffy finished. "Believe me, as much as I would like to, it would be impossible for me to forget about them now."

"I take it from her tone that they are quite serious, academically, that is."

"Quite," Buffy said dryly.

"If you'd like," Giles said, "perhaps I could be of assistance, in some sort of tutoring capacity."

"No time," Buffy said. Then she noticed Oz sitting quietly at the table where Willow usually worked her computer search miracles. "Hey, Oz."

He looked up, seemed a little dazed. "Hey."

He had dark circles under his eyes, his hair seemed even more unkempt than usual, his clothing rumpled. Buffy guessed he probably hadn't slept much if at all. "We'll find her, Oz," Buffy said. "Tonight. I promise."

"Thanks."

"Buffy, I'm afraid we have something else to be concerned about," Giles said.

"Solitaire?"

"Yes, but how did you—oh, of course, but—" Giles

looked down at his book, cleared his throat, looked back at her and shook his head.

"Giles, spill," Buffy said. "I'm too tired to be any more worried."

"I'm afraid it's worse than we imagined," Giles said. "I've found references to a vampire with a terrible history of destruction dating back to Renaissance Italy. He was known by a different name then, *Dies Pedes,* or Day Walker, for his mythic ability to walk in the sun. He sought out and destroyed powerful vampires, who feared him because of this legendary immunity to the rays of the sun. Apparently, a favored tactic of his was to attack them during the day, while they were especially vulnerable."

"So this Day Walker did have access to some sort of magic talisman?"

"The actual mechanism of his invulnerability to sunlight is, I'm afraid, pure speculation."

"What makes you think Solitaire and this Day Walker are one and the same vamp? Maybe Solitaire just found the magic charm in the undead lost and found."

"I cross-checked the journals of two different Watchers spanning a seventy-year period," Giles said. He removed his eyeglasses and massaged the bridge of his nose. "In the first, an extremely distraught Watcher recounted the murder of his Slayer at the hands of *Dies Pedes.* The subsequent journal contains a brief paragraph—speculation really—by a Watcher in his latter years, based upon minimal evidence—well, timetables, method of operation, various comments in the underworld underground that—"

"Cut to the chase, Giles."

"Yes—absolutely," Giles replied, apologetic. "The

short of it is that the second watcher believed *Dies Pedes* became Solitaire, perhaps taking the new name out of a fascination with the one-player card game or simply to reflect his solitary duelist nature. Probably both."

"So this artist formerly known as *Dies Pedes* killed a Slayer?"

"Over three hundred and fifty years ago, yes," Giles replied. "However, there is no further contact with any Slayers. Otherwise, I would have found something sooner."

Buffy had a thought that probably only another Slayer might have. A Slayer or Solitaire himself. It just had a certain . . . clarity. "You know why, don't you?"

"Why what?"

"Why there's been no contact with Slayers in all that time."

"Well, he's been presumed dead for a long time now. I'm not sure what you're—"

"He proved he could do it."

"Do what?"

"Proved he was up to the challenge. The duelist proved he could kill a Slayer," she said. "Been there, done that, time to move on."

"I see," Giles said. "But then why—?"

"Why me? Why now?" Giles nodded. Buffy smiled wryly. "He must think I'm no ordinary Slayer. A special challenge. He wants—"

Oz had been listening all along. Now he stood up. "—a rematch."

"I suppose it makes perfect sense in his worldview," Giles said. "At least we know what you're up against."

"Not feeling comforted," Buffy said.

"If Solitaire really has been around more than five hundred years, living as he has, challenging one powerful vampire after another to duels to the death, he must be incredibly powerful."

Buffy slumped in a chair and shook her head. "I'm starting to think this was a real bad day to skip my Wheaties."

The baroque doors of Angel's mansion rocked with the first impact. The second time Solitaire kicked, they burst open with a crash loud enough to wake the undead. *Well, that is the basic idea,* Solitaire thought. "Honey, I'm home!" he called as he stepped into the great room. *Gotta love the classics.*

"Angel, come out and play!" he called. "It's a beautiful day!"

Silence.

"Need some convincing?" Solitaire crossed to the east side of the great room. "Here, I'll show you!"

As befitted a vampiric abode, heavy draperies covered all the windows. Solitaire tugged down the curtains from the east side window. Sunlight blazed across the room, almost dividing it in half. Dust particles danced in the bright beam, giving it an eerie physicality. Next Solitaire crossed to the opposite window and ripped its curtain down as well. Ambient light brightened the room even more.

Solitaire strode to the fireplace and removed a long poker from the holder beside the mantel. He swung the poker like a baseball bat, admiring the whistling sound it made with each stroke. "Need an alarm clock to get out of bed?" Solitaire called. With his feet spaced wide apart in front of the mantel, he swung the poker inches above the shelf. Any vases, pieces of crystal and sculpture that didn't shatter instantly shot across the room and smashed into the far wall.

Angel appeared in a dark doorway on the other side of the fireplace. He raised the back of his hand to shield his eyes from the unexpectedly bright room. His gaze lingered warily on the shafts of light slicing through the room. The floor was now a patchwork design of light and dark, where the light sections would be as lethal to him as lava. Yet the floor was the simplest part of the three-dimensional trap. The air, crisscrossed with beams of light, felt as if it were electrified. Angel's skin practically itched at the nearness of the sun's rays.

"Ah, the sleeper awakes," Solitaire said as he walked about carelessly, sunlight rippling up his black slacks, red vest and topcoat as he moved from one area to the next. His hands blazed with light but did not burn. Likewise his face remained unblemished by exposure to the light of day.

"Get out," Angel said.

"Not so fast," Solitaire said, purposely stopping in the middle of the widest shaft of light. "I hear you and the Slayer are quite close."

"Stay away from Buffy," Angel said, his jaw flexed as he ground his teeth together. For the moment, it was an empty threat. Angel was helpless as long as Solitaire waited in the light.

"I've waited long enough."

"It's not gonna happen."

Solitaire chuckled. "I would like you—the pet vampire—to deliver a message to Buffy," Solitaire said, slapping the end of the poker into his open palm. "I'm afraid it's a very painful message."

"I'm sorry, Giles. It would be way too painful in your present condition," Buffy had said when she saw her Watcher waiting for her in the library during her study period wearing his padded suit, the one designed to protect the wearer during attack dog training or, in their situation, Slayer training. Concerned that fatigue and worrying over her missing friends would dull her reflexes, Giles had suggested she incorporate a workout into her study period. What she hadn't known was that he planned to fire questions at her mind while she fired fists, elbows and feet at his—mostly protected—body. Buffy had no intention of adding further injuries to those already inflicted on her Watcher by Solitaire.

"Perhaps you make a good point," Giles had conceded, nudging his eyeglasses up the bridge of his nose. With his padded gloves on, the minute adjustment had looked about as awkward and comical as attempting to play the piano while wearing oven mitts. "I'll get the heavy bag."

While Giles had brought out the specially rigged punching bag, Buffy had changed into a crop top, loose sweat pants and sneakers. For the past fifteen minutes, she'd been pounding the bag with a series of kicks and combination punches, any one of which probably would have taken a heavyweight boxer down for the count. It had been a quick way for her to purge the enormous amount of nervous energy that had been building in her since Willow and then Xander had gone missing. And she'd even managed to successfully answer several of the sample test questions Giles had thrown her way.

"That felt good," Buffy said, slightly out of breath. Her face, arms and bare midriff were covered in a healthy sheen of sweat as she danced nimbly on the balls of her feet to keep her muscles loose. "You don't know how bad I've been itching to pound something."

Giles had removed and stored his padded suit during her warm-ups. He cleared his throat. "In retrospect, may I say I'm most appreciative you declined my services as punching bag."

"Never kick a man when he's down," Buffy said. "Now, vampires on the other hand . . ."

"Would it therefore be safe for me to inquire about this morning's calculus exam?"

"Calculus was derivative," Buffy said with a grin.

"Ah," Giles said, noting her humor. "So I suppose your upcoming history exam will be—"

"Repetitious," Buffy replied. "Although the poor grades will not be repeating themselves. Power of positive thinking."

"Well, I must say, you're in a much better mood."

"One test down, one to go." Buffy shadowboxed three quick jabs, then lashed out with a shoulder-high kick. "All the waiting and worrying was driving me crazy. But tonight—" She dropped to a crouch, palms flat on the tiles, and snapped her heel out with enough force to shatter a demon's kneecap. Assuming, of course, the imaginary demon actually had a kneecap. Some of them lacked caps, knees and all. Buffy stood, hands triumphantly planted on her hips. "Tonight we find Willow and Xander, after which I intend to make goulash out of a few marginally talented ghouls."

"You must not forget about Solitaire."

Buffy pounded her right fist into her left palm. "If he knows what's good for him," Buffy said, invigorated with renewed confidence, "Solitaire will get on the next bus out of my town."

Solitaire walked casually out of the light, swinging the poker overhead like it was an ax and he was splitting firewood. Angel lunged forward, keeping in relative darkness as he caught the brass shaft in his hands and tried to pull it from Solitaire's grasp. Solitaire was expecting that tactic and shoved it toward Angel, causing him to lose his balance. Next he swept the poker in a circle, using Angel's momentum to spin him around toward the light.

At the last moment, Angel let go of the poker to avoid the beam of light. He'd come too close. It felt as if an oven door had been opened right behind him. Solitaire had no such constraint. He took the direct path and clubbed Angel with the poker as he staggered back toward the mantel. The sharp metal tip of the poker dug into Angel's shoulder, tearing the cloth of his shirt. Angel growled, sprouting his fangs and vampface.

He picked up a heavy armchair and hurled it at Solitaire. Solitaire dropped his poker as he swatted the chair aside. Even as Angel dove for the poker, Solitaire sprang forward and kicked it across the floor, where it slid into a patch of light. Pulling up short, Angel stood just outside the light—until Solitaire shoved him into it.

Startled, Angel nevertheless rolled with the shove,

tucking into a somersault even as flames began to erupt on his face and hands, his clothes smoking and dangerously close to combustion. One hand shot out and grabbed the heavy curtains Solitaire had torn from the window and pulled them over his body like a cloak, while the other arm managed to grab the poker as he rolled back up into a standing position beyond the light. Panting, he smothered the hot spots that prickled all over his body with the heavy, musty curtains. But the pain and the real danger of combustion proved a fateful distraction.

Solitaire strode right through the light and lashed out with a side kick beneath Angel's solar plexus, slamming him into the wall. Next he gripped the shaft of the poker in both hands and spun Angel around, toward the light once again. Hands already numb from burns, Angel relented and released the poker, spinning awkwardly on his heel to hop away from the light. The curtain he'd draped over his back spun free, casting a fleeting shelter of darkness until it fluttered to the floor.

With a low, one-armed swing of the poker, Solitaire caught Angel behind the right knee, which was supporting all his weight, and tugged. Angel toppled over, slapping his palms to the floor to catch himself even as the back of his head felt as if it were inches from a blowtorch. He twisted away from the sunlight that had almost ignited his hair, rolled across the floor away from the east side of the great room where the sunlight was the most direct and the deadliest.

Solitaire followed mercilessly, clubbing Angel across the thigh, then the bicep. His steel-toed leather boot slammed into the small of Angel's back, causing him to bend backward in agony. Spinning the poker like a police baton, Solitaire struck Angel across the chin, then back across the forehead, splitting open his scalp. Angel raised a forearm in defense and felt it crack as the poker came down hard across the bone.

Laughing, Solitaire clutched and twisted Angel's damaged arm, using it to pull him across the floor, toward the east windows. Angel groaned, clenching his jaw against the pain and reached up with his other hand to grab Solitaire's arm. The poker lashed out again, striking him in the face. His vision grayed again but he clung desperately to consciousness. It was an uneven playing field, but somehow he had to find a way to stop Solitaire before he went after Buffy.

Angel's back grew painfully hot, his shirt smoldering while Solitaire held him a hairsbreadth away from the sunlight. Acrid smoke filled his nostrils. He gritted his teeth, gnashed his fangs, but his legs refused to support his weight. He thought the right one might even be broken. His arms felt leaden as well. Somehow the pain helped him focus, look for some opportunity to turn the tables.

"Good," Solitaire said, breathing heavily despite that infuriating smile. "I have your attention."

"Stay away from Buffy," Angel whispered.

"You just don't get it, do you?" Solitaire's brow contorted in vampiric folds as he bared an impressive set of fangs. "Maybe a bit of fresh air will do the trick."

Solitaire dragged Angel toward the doors of the mansion, toward daylight. Angel went limp, forcing Solitaire to drop the poker and support Angel's weight with both hands.

"Wait . . ." Angel said softly, with an air of defeat.

Solitaire paused just before the light spilling through the entrance. "You're right," Solitaire said. "If I let the sun burn you to ashes, there won't be enough left to deliver my message. I'll say this just once. You ready?"

"Ready," Angel said. And viciously head-butted Solitaire, whose nose crumpled under Angel's forehead.

Solitaire roared in anger and heaved Angel backward, which was exactly where he wanted to go. But Angel hadn't allowed for his lame right leg and, as he leaped toward the gleaming poker, his knee buckled and he fell hard. Solitaire leapt right on top of Angel, grinding his heels into Angel's back for good measure before stepping down to scoop up the poker.

Angel reached for the only thing in his grasp, caught Solitaire's heel and yanked it hard, bringing him down. But Solitaire swung the poker in both hands even as he fell. The sharp, hooked end whistled toward Angel's face with enough force to flay the skin off his skull. Angel recoiled, twisting his head to the side, avoiding all but a glancing blow to his forehead. This time everything went completely black.

Angel blinked his eyes open a moment later and was looking up into Solitaire's enraged but triumphant face. Solitaire's nose was swollen, a trickle of dark blood oozing from a lacerated nostril. His fist was wrapped tightly in the cloth of Angel's torn and bloody shirt, bunched at the collar, his knuckles pressing into Angel's throat. "You lose," Solitaire hissed. "Now the message. It's simple, really. Just two words, so I know you won't forget it. Tell the Slayer . . . she's next."

Solitaire was gone.

Angel stared up toward the ceiling, not really seeing anything. The pain was a living thing, working its way throughout his body, finding more and more interesting places to torment.

At some point, the beams of sunlight intersecting the room shifted enough to find him in his small island of darkness. One of his trouser legs started to smoke, the skin beneath it sizzling. The smell, more than the pain, alerted him. He rolled over and crawled facedown, inching his way toward the fireplace, collapsing where the cool darkness seemed deepest.

One word rose up from his throat, escaped his lips. "Buffy. . . ."

CHAPTER 12

At dusk, the four ghouls who comprised Vyxn finally left their run-down house, leaving Willow and Xander alone. The first thing Willow said was, "Don't suppose you have any more chocolate?"

Xander shook his head. "If I had known it was a sleepover, I would have stocked up." He coiled his legs and attempted to roll backward, inadvertently slamming his head into the wall. "If that looked like it hurt, it's because it did."

"What were you trying to do?"

"Something I saw on TV," Xander said. "Slip the manacles under my legs to get my hands in front of me."

"Let me see," Willow said and examined his manacles and the chain that bound them together. "There's a problem."

"What? I'm not limber enough?"

"No," Willow said. "Not enough slack in the chain. Unless you could do one leg at a time."

"Definitely not limber enough for that." He sighed. "The ghouls probably watched the same TV shows and made their chains shorter."

"They're sneaky that way," Willow agreed, dejected.

"Hey, Will, why don't you try? You're smaller than me and, I'm betting, more limber."

Just before leaving to perform their final show, the ghouls had decided to manacle Willow's hands behind her back as well. "There," Lupa had said. "That should keep both of you out of trouble." And Xander had replied, "Just not out of ghoul trouble." Carnie had laughed and said, "You're cute enough to eat—which is kind of the whole idea."

"Okay," Willow said. "I can be Limber Girl." She brought her knees up to her chest and rocked back, straining her arms. She tried twice before she stretched far enough to slip the chain under her heels. Standing in triumph, she held her manacled hands up before her. "Voilà!"

"Great, Will! You did it!"

"Refresh my memory," Willow said, the corners of her smile slipping. "What do I do now that my arms are chained in front of me instead of behind me?"

"When the Nazi guard returns, you jump up and wrap the chain around his neck, rendering him unconscious. Then we take his keys, unlock the chains and one of us, probably me, puts on his uniform—which will be a perfect fit—to catch the other guards by surprise."

"You realize there are no Nazi guards?"

"Yeah, well, I hadn't thought that far ahead."

Willow walked to the board mounted on the wall, examined the ring her collar chain had been passed through.

"Try to turn it," Xander suggested.

"I already tried," Willow explained. "Before they brought you. Not enough leverage."

"What about your secret bag of magic tricks?" Xander asked. "Any good spells for breaking chains? Picking locks?"

Willow sighed. "I tried a spell on the lock but nothing happened. Oh—but I did figure out how to make the chains rattle on their own."

"What good did that do?"

"Gave me the willies," Willow remarked with a shiver. "I even tried turning the wall ring magically, but there's too much resistance. It's screwed in so tight all I managed was to give myself a splitting headache."

"So brute force is called for," Xander said. He stood on tiptoes next to his ring, reaching awkwardly up with both hands still manacled behind his back. He managed a clumsy grip on the ring but couldn't budge it. "All we need is a crowbar."

Willow looked around. "Fresh out of crowbars."

"Damn," Xander said and slammed his foot into the drywall. "We could probably kick the house down and we'd still be chained to this board."

He walked as far as the collar chain would let him roam. Not enough slack to reach the boarded up windows or the door, which hung partially askew from the damaged doorframe. Willow had already sat back down and was staring at the crude manacles. Xander sighed and walked back to join her.

"If I had a bobby pin I could pick the locks," Willow said.

"Really? You could do that?"

"Well, it doesn't seem all that hard on TV," she said and managed a grin.

"What are we gonna do, Will?"

"Wait for Buffy," Willow said.

Xander sighed. "So much for my fragile male ego," he said. "Don't you know it's my job to rescue the fair damsel from the"—he examined their surroundings, the stained walls, exposed plaster and boarded-up windows—"condemned tower?"

"You really think so?" Willow said, quirking a smile.

"Right there on page sixteen of the *Chivalry Guide*," Xander said. "Under 'Rescues and Narrow Escapes.' "

"No," Willow said. "I mean the part about me—you know—the fair damsel. 'Fair' being secret medieval code for pretty."

"Right," Xander said.

"So you think I'm pretty," Willow said, lifting her chin.

"Of course I do, Will," Xander said.

"It's just that, you never really said it, you know, like, 'Hi, Willow, you know, you're really pretty.' "

"Some of us chivalrous knights are also tied of tongue," Xander said.

"So you *think* it?" Willow pressed. "Even if you never say it?"

"Sure, Will, but, us being best buds and all, there are rules and procedures about the not saying of the mushy stuff."

"Oh, I understand," Willow said, looking down at her

manacles again. "And it's not like I don't have Oz for the saying of the mushy stuff."

"Oz is a great guy," Xander said. "He's worried sick about you, you know."

"Poor Oz," Willow said. "Wonder if I'll ever see him again."

"We've been in worse jams," Xander said, trying for upbeat. "Just don't ask me to name any right this moment."

"Thank you, Xander," Willow said. "For what it's worth, I think you're a great guy too."

The room had become darker, the last rays of the sun no longer squeezing through the gaps in the plywood nailed across the windows. Already Willow could barely make out Xander's face. And with the approach of the new moon, their faint hopes seemed to quiver on the edge of extinction like the coming of the night.

"Buffy will be hooking up with Angel by now," Xander said.

"And Oz," Willow added. She felt awful knowing Oz was so worried about her, ached with the need to tell him she was okay. *Okay, for now.* "They'll find us, Xander. I know they will."

Xander nodded, an almost imperceptible gesture in the gathering gloom. Somehow she knew Xander didn't trust his voice to utter an optimistic thought with any conviction. Willow had her own, unvoiced doubts. *Even if Buffy somehow finds us, the ghouls are expecting her.* As much as she hated to admit it, the Scooby Gang was in big trouble.

"Angel!" Buffy whispered, alarmed. From a distance, she noticed the doors to the mansion had been damaged.

As she moved closer, she saw the large footprint cracked into the surface of the wood, the jagged splinters where the lock had given way. Someone had kicked in the doors. And she was all too afraid she knew who it had been. She stood outside the door, listening for any sound within, but the pounding of her heart was all she heard.

Placing the side of her palm against the door, she eased it inward just enough to allow her to slip through the gap. Her other hand had already plucked a wooden stake from her backpack. Gloom filled the great room, but the street light that bled through called her attention to the bare windows . . . and the rumpled curtains beneath them.

A faint groan sounded from across the room, drawing her gaze to the dark shape huddled inside the wide fireplace. "Angel," Buffy called. A raspy voice called back to her, unintelligible. But recognizable. She rushed to his side, putting the stake back into her bag. Whatever had happened here, it was long over.

Angel had been curled in a fetal position, knees drawn up to his chest, forearms pressed against his face. Upon hearing her voice, he started to move his arms and legs. His clothing was torn and streaked with blood where it hadn't been scorched. Wherever his flesh was exposed, it was covered with angry red welts where, she imagined, blisters had formed and already healed. Buffy examined the layout of the room again and realized he must have crawled to this one spot, avoiding the penetrating rays of the sunlight while his body attempted to recover from devastating injuries.

On the floor near Angel's feet, almost unnoticed in the gloom, was a playing card. A nine of spades. *Solitaire,*

Buffy thought bitterly. Her vision blurred with the welling of tears. Her fists were clenched so tight they had begun to tremble. She longed to touch Angel, to comfort him, but what could she do for him that his accelerated vampiric healing could not? In a way, she was almost responsible. Angel had been attacked by Solitaire to taunt her, the Slayer.

"Solitaire," Angel said.

"I know," Buffy replied. "He came here to fight you, using sunlight as a weapon so the odds would be clearly in his favor." She pressed her face close to him, her blond hair fanning across his reddened face. "Angel, it's safe now," she said. "The sun has set."

"Not safe"—Angel said, his voice raw—"for you. He's coming for you next."

"I'll worry about Solitaire later," Buffy said. "Tell me how I can help you." But she already knew the answer.

"Packets," he said. "Refrigerator."

Packets. Of blood. She nodded and went for his sustenance. Even though he had a soul and a conscience, he still had the needs of a vampire. Blood being first and foremost among them.

She helped him at first, but after a few ounces he sat up and turned his back to her, self-conscious, while he finished the first packet. Buffy retreated to a stuffed armchair, chin on her palms, elbows on her knees while he finished a second packet and a third. Her face was lined only with concern, not the disgust she knew he imagined she felt. They had been through too much together for his blood-thirst to bother her.

He inhaled deeply and climbed to his feet. Buffy rose

to help him as his legs wobbled, but he held out a hand to stop her, using the other hand to grip the mantel. He wanted to prove to her he could take care of himself . . . because he wanted to be there for her.

"Angel, I—"

"No," Angel said. "I'm okay now."

"You don't look—"

"I'm a vampire, remember," Angel said. "I heal fast. I'll be fine. Soon." He rubbed a spot on his neck that was raw, wincing at the flare of pain. "Besides, it's night now. He's lost his advantage."

"So it really is true," Buffy said. "He's . . . immune to the sun."

"Definitely," Angel responded.

While Angel composed himself, walking in slow circles to test his bruised and burnt legs, Buffy explained Giles's discovery that Solitaire and *Dies Pedes*—the Day Walker—were one and the same vampire.

Angel shook his head. "I'd heard rumors about a day-walking vampire, hundreds of years ago, but I never believed it. Vampires just don't walk around in the sunlight. I thought it was, for lack of a better term, an urban legend. Just a myth."

"To scare the little vampire children?" Buffy said, but Angel wasn't smiling at her attempt at humor. "All the Watcher books and journals can't be wrong, can they?"

Angel shook his head. Images of Solitaire blithely walking through shafts of direct sunlight haunted him. "Whatever he is, he's dangerous."

"Well, it was hardly a fair fight," Buffy said, indicating the bare windows.

"Even if we had fought at night," Angel said. He looked directly at her with that penetrating gaze that could give her shivers for all the right and all the wrong reasons. "Buffy, Solitaire is powerful. Don't underestimate him."

"Don't worry about me, Angel," Buffy said, standing up from the chair. "I'll be more than ready for him when he shows his ugly face, if he ever shows his ugly face. Right now, though, I have to think about Willow and Xander. This is our last chance to track the ghouls back to their lair."

"And you want my help."

"Of course," Buffy replied. "But that was before . . . this. You should stay here, get better—"

"No. I'll come."

Buffy was just as glad to have him close by. If he was close to her, she could protect him. Her friends had fallen into trouble when they were separated from her. She couldn't—wouldn't—let that happen again. *Those who do not remember the past are condemned to relive it.* There, she'd learned something about history, after all. And she recalled reading on a motivational poster in Mrs. Burzak's office that the Chinese definition of insanity was to do the same thing over and over and expect different results. "Good," was all she said to Angel.

He nodded. "What's the plan?"

Inside the Bronze, Vyxn was performing the second set of the last night of their special engagement. Cordelia Chase looked over the excited throng of male concertgoers and shook her head. *Never underestimate the male libido,* was her first thought. *Definitely a two-bib minimum for these droolers,* was her second. Though she supposed there was something more at work, if what Buffy, Oz and Giles had told her was true, that the band members really were flesh-eating ghouls with the ability to mesmerize guys.

Cordelia noticed a few, almost token, girls in the audience, uniformly ignored by their dates, all of whom had eyes only for the four female *whatevers* on stage. As a former card-carrying member of the Scooby Gang, Cordelia accepted that in Sunnydale coincidence often meant danger and skepticism was best reserved for the foolish or naive. So she was more than willing to *not* accept Vyxn at face value. Against her better judgment, she found herself participating in the stake-out. While there was still a chance—however small—that Troy was still alive, she should be there ready to help. After all, he'd promised her a screen test. How would it look if she abandoned him the moment things became a little dicey. *An ounce of loyalty is worth a ton of referrals.*

Giles had assured her that she would be immune to the power the ghoul's music had over men. But that just meant she was forced to sit through the sappy love ballads and woman-scorned tunes on their own dubious merit. Meanwhile the guys had a free pass, waiting in Oz's van. Giles had never heard the band himself but feared succumbing to the siren song. Oz had said he still felt a compulsion to hear the band, even knowing what he knew about them. As a vampire, Angel seemed unaffected—the ghouls probably never developed a taste for raw vampire flesh—but he was basically a mess, still a little gimpy from an earlier battle with Super Vampire. *So, fine for the guys, but why does little Miss Slayer get to skip the terrible tunes?* Buffy should be here suffering right alongside her.

Oz drummed his fingers on the steering wheel of his van. *It's almost over,* he kept telling himself. Just a little while longer, until the end of Vyxn's performance, and then he could help rescue Willow. From his driver's seat he could see Vyxn's van, fifty yards away but cloaked in deep shadows. Tugging at him was the irrational fear that the rust-colored van would slip away unnoticed or simply vanish like a mirage. So he stared, waiting for the slightest bit of movement.

Giles tried to think about anything to keep his mind off the itch under his cast, the itch just maddeningly out of reach of the six-inch ruler he'd brought along. He watched the door of the Bronze, wondering when Cordelia would come out to tell them the band was wrapping up its last performance although, from what he'd been told, he expected they would play until eleven o'clock. More out of curiosity than anything else, he wondered what it would be like to listen to Vyxn's music. Still, he didn't trust himself enough to sample it. He thought of Ulysses, who had had himself tied to the mast of his ship so he might hear the siren song, yet not succumb to its power. Mostly, Giles prayed for the safety of Willow and Xander. Even though they had become—for want of a better term—Slayerettes of their own choosing, he still felt responsible for them and dared not entertain the thought that it might already be too late.

If all that weren't enough, Giles also worried about Buffy's chances against Solitaire. Angel had clearly had the worst of their battle. Obviously the day-walking vampire considered another vampire much more of a worthy opponent than a middle-aged Watcher. Giles supposed he should be grateful that Solitaire considered him harmless. Still, it irked him. Made him question his worth to his Slayer, to Buffy.

Buffy had been keeping an eye on Angel, worried that he would be too vulnerable to face the ghouls in battle or a return visit from Solitaire. And it was hard for her to keep the concern out of her face every time she looked at him. She spoke softly, to spare his feelings in front of the others. "Angel? Are you up for this?"

He took the question seriously, nodded slowly. "The bones have knit and the burns are just a little tender. I'm fine, just—sore as hell."

"You should know, I guess," Buffy said. "Since you've actually been there."

Angel winced and Buffy instantly regretted her flippant remark. She kept trying to make light of his condition to hide her deep concern. Solitaire had come within inches—literally—of killing Angel by exposing him to direct sunlight. Angel still seemed a little wobbly and tentative when he walked, despite his claim that his bones were completely healed. Buffy decided a topic change was in order. "So, any tips for me? Just in case Solitaire finally does come after me and not just the people I care about."

"He's strong," Angel said. "Incredibly strong. And bold. He uses his advantages for maximum benefit, to tip the odds in his favor."

Buffy frowned. "So, in the weaknesses column, I'm marking down a big 'not applicable'?"

"Ego," Angel said.

"Ego?" Buffy asked. "Meaning, what? I should ask for his autograph before I stake him?"

"Overconfidence," Angel explained. "He takes great pride in his superiority."

Buffy nodded. "So, the bigger they come . . ."

"The harder they fall on you," Oz interjected with a quick backward glance . "Sorry, I—"

Two explosive impacts rocked the van.

"The roof!" Angel shouted.

A dark shape leapt down from the dented roof to the passenger side of the van a moment before a second figure landed on the driver's side. At the first sign of trouble, Buffy had leaned over the front seat of the van. She looked left and right, then did a double take. "Twins?"

Two identical vampires stood on either side of the van, in full vampface, each wearing black trousers and a red leather vest.

Buffy shot a glance at Angel, but he shook his head. He'd never seen them before. But the red vests seemed to indicate some affiliation with Solitaire.

"I'm Kyle," said the vampire on Oz's side as he whipped open the door.

"I'm Carl," said the other as he yanked open Giles's door.

Kyle grabbed a startled Oz by the collar and threw him to the ground, while his twin pulled Giles from the van. Giles swept his cast up as he fell and managed to smash Carl's nose.

"Come out, Slayer!" Kyle yelled. "We have a message for you!"

CHAPTER 13

Buffy was way ahead of the vampire twins. She was over the front seat even as Giles hit the ground, a wooden stake already in her hand. Carl made the mistake of examining his busted nose. By the time he looked up, Buffy was on him, stake driving forward.

"Wait—!" he screamed a moment before it pierced his heart and he burst into a cloud of vamp dust.

Buffy circled around the front of the van. "Time to double my fun," she said, moving closer to the remaining twin, Kyle.

"You killed Carl," Kyle said in disbelief.

"Don't be jealous," she said. "You're next."

"Wait," he said, holding up his hands, palms out. "We— I mean, I have a message for you."

"Enough with the messages," Buffy said.

Oz had climbed to his feet and positioned himself behind Kyle, but some small movement or sound alerted the vampire, who whirled around and drove an elbow into Oz, just below his rib cage. Oz doubled over, the wind knocked out of him, but Buffy was quick to take advantage of the distraction. She sprang forward and caught the vampire in the face with a stinging left hook. As he shook it off, she grabbed the front of his vest in her left hand and raised the wooden stake high in her right, determined to put a quick end to Kyle. She thrust the stake toward his unbeating heart—

"Your mother!" Kyle screamed.

—and pulled the fatal blow at the last instant.

"He has your mother," Kyle finished, eyes wide with fear.

"Solitaire?"

Kyle nodded vigorously, his gaze trained on the sharp point of the stake.

Buffy couldn't afford not to believe him. She had to find out everything this vampire knew. Her mother's life probably depended on it. When she thought how close she'd come to dusting him without discovering Solitaire's terms, she shuddered. Her throat was constricted, her voice harsh. "She's still alive?"

"Yes, as far as I—"

"Where?"

"He told us to leave you to him. Just deliver his message and get lost."

"Where?" Buffy repeated, pressing the stake against his chest.

"The gallery," Kyle said. "He said he would take her to the gallery."

"Anything else?"

"Come alone or she dies," the vampire blurted. "If you don't show by midnight, he kills her anyway. That's all I know."

"You're sure about that? Absolutely positive?"

"Yes! Absolutely!"

"Thanks for the message," Buffy said. "Here's your tip!"

"Nooo!!!" Kyle screamed, realizing too late she was being literal. His hands—along with the rest of him—turned to dust long before he could deflect the wooden stake.

Angel had helped Oz up and stood with him to the left behind Buffy. Giles brushed himself off as he approached her from the right. "I hesitate to call that completely unsportsmanlike—"

"Good," Buffy said. "You don't think I'd leave a vamp on the loose simply because he cooperated?"

Giles cleared his throat. "Quite right."

"You all heard?" Buffy asked. "Solitaire has my mom at the gallery." They nodded and she could see the concern in their expressions, probably worried as much for her as for her mother.

"If we leave now, we risk losing Vyxn and any chance of finding Willow and Xander," Giles added.

"Dilemma in a nutshell," Oz remarked.

"No dilemma," Buffy replied. "I'm going to the gallery alone."

"Buffy, that's precisely what he—"

"Giles, you heard his terms. I can't—I won't risk my mother's life."

"I understand."

"Good," Buffy said to her Watcher. She held her hand out, palm up. "I need your keys. I'm taking the Gilesmobile."

"Buffy, automobiles aren't your—perhaps we should—"

"No time to argue, Giles."

"All right then," Giles said, dropping the keys to his Citroën in her hand. "Do be careful—that is, with Solitaire and everything."

"Find Vyxn's lair and wait for me as long as you can," Buffy said. "Giles, you and Oz are vulnerable to Vyxn's spell and that would leave Angel alone against the four of them. Worse if they can somehow turn both of you against him."

"How will you know where—?"

"Have Cordelia follow you in her car," Buffy said. "Once she knows the location, she comes back to the Bronze and waits for me. Everyone clear?"

Angel said, "Buffy, I could—"

She was already shaking her head. "If Solitaire or one of his vampire cronies sees you, he might kill my mom. I can't risk that. Besides, these guys are outnumbered by the ghouls. They *need* you. And I can't risk you coming with me."

Angel nodded once.

Buffy managed to drive Giles's Citroën to the gallery without incident, unless one counted a rude encounter with a curb and a popped hubcap as incidents. She could still picture the strained look on Angel's face, not wanting to let her fight Solitaire alone but yielding to her logic and the threat to her mother. Also weighing on her mind was the real possibility that Solitaire could kill her, leaving her battered friends to face the ghouls alone. Yet she tried to put these distractions out of her mind as she neared the art gallery. If Solitaire was as powerful as Giles's history books and Angel's assertions, she would need to be completely focused to fight him. Still . . . he had her mother.

A disturbing thought rose from her subconscious. Her mother had been home when she left for the Bronze. Had Solitaire somehow thwarted the uninvite spell she'd performed on her house? She was sure she had done it properly. *Why am I so surprised?* she thought. If a vampire can walk in daylight, why would entering a house uninvited be so extraordinary? Maybe he did have access to a powerful talisman or some special magic. She had no clear explanation for his abilities, but she was determined not to underestimate her opponent. *Solitaire is no ordinary vampire.*

Too restless to simply sit at a table and listen to Vyxn's uninspired music, Cordelia walked rather aimlessly around the back of the Bronze, trying to pass the time. At least until a freshman in rumpled clothing bumped into her, almost spilling his soda on her red dress. Pale-faced, with dark rings under his eyes, he sported a slack-jawed look of confusion. He mumbled an apology and tried to step around her.

"Watch it, geek!" Cordelia snapped. "Try some No Doz."

So incensed was Cordelia that she barely noticed when Lupa, onstage, said, "Gotta leave early tonight, guys." A collective moan of disappointment. "You've been great."

The sunken-eyed freshman mumbled some more and stumbled away, veering closer to the stage, a moth drawn to the light. Cordelia took a few moments to examine nearby faces and realized they all had that vacant, sleep-is-for-losers, mesmerized look. If Vyxn extended their engagement a few days, the guys would probably collapse from exhaustion. Not only were the ghouls eating some of their fans, they were apparently sucking the life out of the rest of them.

". . . our last song," Lupa was saying, just as Cordelia noticed the dark spots. The mumbling freshman bumbler *had* managed to spill some of his Coke on her dress.

". . . called 'Farewell, Again, Forever.' "

"Great," Cordelia said and made a beeline for the ladies' room to inspect the damage.

Thunderous cheers and applause faded as Lupa walked to the middle of the stage and began to sing her final number.

"If I never see you again,
will you remember me?
Our time was so short,
but that's the way it must be . . ."

It was a trap and Buffy was about to step into it. Not that she had any choice. Her mother's life was in danger, so she must risk her own. Joyce would never want her daughter to place herself in danger to save her. But

Buffy wasn't just Joyce Summers's daughter, she was the Chosen One, the Slayer. Born to fight in the battle against evil and to someday—when the odds finally caught up to her—die in that battle. *Just not today,* Buffy thought. Buffy refused to let her mother become a casualty in her war.

After parking the Citroën a block from her mother's art gallery, Buffy proceeded on foot, carrying the weapons she'd taken from the van, a crossbow, quarrels and a wooden stake. First priority: get her mother out safely. Second priority: give Solitaire a very personal introduction to Mr. Pointy. Then back to the Bronze where, she hoped, Cordelia would be waiting to take her to the ghouls' lair in time to save her friends, Willow and Xander. She prayed they were still alive. *Hold on, guys.* She sighed. *First things first.*

Her mother's car was parked slightly askew, outside the gallery, its front tire scuffed by the curb. Solitaire had made Joyce Summers drive here knowing she was being used as bait to lure her daughter, her only child, to her death. Buffy was determined to make Solitaire pay—for breaking Giles's wrist, for attacking Angel and for terrorizing her mother. All his debts were long overdue.

The door to the gallery was unlocked. Buffy took a moment to peer through the glass, into the darkness, attempting to locate either her mother or Solitaire. The glare of streetlights only partially illuminated the interior of the gallery but, from the inside, Buffy would be silhouetted, plain to see. As she reached for the door handle, she noticed the playing card on the welcome mat at her feet. Eight of hearts. Turn an eight on its side and it was the symbol for infinity. But she doubted there was any deeper meaning to Solitaire's playing card affectation. He was just working his way through the deck. *This time you lose, Solitaire.*

Though she pulled the door open with as much care as possible, the crystal chimes tinkled overhead. So much for whatever tiny element of surprise she might have had. She eased the door shut behind her.

A suit of armor stood mute guard next to the door, a double-headed battle-ax balanced under gleaming metal gauntlets, blade resting on the floor. Buffy recalled her mother discussing a medieval exhibit. For one creepy moment, she entertained the thought that Solitaire was even now inside the suit of armor. Wouldn't it be ironic, she thought, if Solitaire had actually been alive when knights of old wore such contraptions during their battles, tourneys and jousts? Maybe that was how and when he'd developed his taste for competition and duels.

To her left, the wall was adorned with mounted weapons and shields of the period, some merely reproductions or approximations. On the opposite wall—above a row of display cases filled with actual six-hundred-year-old antiquities or clever replicas—were prints of artwork from the period. The one nearest the entrance she recognized as *The Triumph of Death*, from the fourteenth century. Above a plague scene with decomposing corpses laid out in coffins, angels and demons fought over the souls of the dead. She had seen a reproduction of the painting in one of Giles's books and the macabre image had stuck with her.

A muffled moan came from across the main exhibition room. Buffy's gaze was drawn to the sight of her mother, bound and gagged, as she sat in deep shadows, propped up against the wall. Her mother's eyes were wide with fright, and she tilted her head to the side, indicating the other corner of the room, which was cloaked in almost complete darkness.

Solitaire stepped out of that darkness, into the wan glow cast by the streetlights. In his black cloak and trousers, only his red leather vest and pale face were clearly outlined. He almost seemed to float in the gloom, an apparition or a demon waiting to collect his bounty of souls. "We meet at last, Slayer," he said in a deep, confident voice.

"You're the one who's been hiding," Buffy said to irritate him, hoping it would throw him off his game. She was thinking, *I need to get Mom out of here now.*

"Well, the preliminaries are over," Solitaire said, spreading his hands expansively. "Everything has been prepared for our contest. Before I trussed her up, I had your mother disarm the security system so we wouldn't be interrupted by the police. Nothing like bumbling local law enforcement to ruin the aesthetics of a spectacular duel. We have the place all to ourselves, for as long as it takes. I suggest we make the most of it."

"I have a message for you," Buffy said. She had slung a crossbow over her back, but now she brought it to bear. "Don't worry, I'll get right to the point." She fired the bolt.

Solitaire's hand was a blur of motion as he snatched the quarrel out of the air, inches from his chest. "Ha! A sense of humor," he said and chuckled. "I love it. Do you think you'll die with a smile on your face, Slayer?" He snapped the quarrel in half and tossed it aside.

"If I do," Buffy said, loading a second bolt, "you won't be around to see it." She fired again.

Solitaire's arm swept up in a half circle and the deflected quarrel lodged in a wall behind him. "Confident," he remarked. "Good. This grows tiresome. Shall we begin?"

"First, let my mother go," Buffy said. She had hoped to put a quick end to Solitaire, but now realized things were going to get ugly. "She has nothing to do with this. She's no threat to you."

"She stays," Solitaire replied. "After all, a mother should have the chance to witness her daughter die a glorious death."

Buffy had to think about her mother first, no matter what happened to her. Solitaire prided himself on being a warrior. Maybe she could play on his honor. "In the unlikely event you . . . beat me, promise you'll let her go."

"Why should I do that?"

"It would be . . . honorable."

"After our little dance, I fear I might be . . . thirsty."

"You're scum," Buffy said. *He's a vampire. What was I expecting, a great humanitarian?*

"This is a fight to the death," Solitaire said. "Yet you resort to name calling?" Solitaire reached into a vest pocket and pulled out a playing card. He showed it to her: a seven of spades. "Consider this your grave marker." He laid it face up on one of the display cases to his left. "Now that you're sufficiently motivated," he said, "let's see what you're made of, Slayer."

"Time for a little vamp dusting," Buffy said and

charged. She flung the empty crossbow at him, simultaneously reaching into her pocket for a wooden stake.

Solitaire leaned to the side, letting the crossbow whistle past his head and stood his ground. His attention stayed focused on the stake Buffy held high in her right hand. Knowing he'd expect a quick thrust, Buffy cartwheeled, planting her free hand on the floor and drilling both feet into Solitaire's chest. He staggered backward as she righted herself and pressed her attack. This time she drove the stake down toward his chest. He blocked her wrist with his forearm, then slammed his open palm under her chin, lifting her off her feet. Buffy lost her balance and started to fall. She grabbed his vest with her left hand as she fell back, using gravity and his own momentum against him. Her back hit the floor a moment before her head struck hard, stars flashing in a painful moment of darkness. But she planted a foot in his abdomen as she continued to roll and hurled him over her body. He crashed to the floor with a grunt, while Buffy rolled over onto her hands and knees.

She had a momentary advantage and willed herself not to lose it. Running toward him, she drove a knee into his face even as he climbed to his feet. He roared in pain, but swung his fist in a wild arc that connected with her ear, crushing cartilage and splitting the skin open. Blood began to trickle down her neck.

Buffy took a step back, trying to catch her breath. Solitaire rose, towering above her. He launched a side-kick that she caught in both hands but lost her stake in the process. She twisted hard, attempting to throw him to the ground. Time enough then to retrieve the stake. But she forgot his inhuman nature, he spun in a complete arc, seemingly defying gravity as he pulled his leg free of her grasp. Seeing her guard down, he backhanded her across the face, whipping her head to the side with the impact. Then he rushed her and caught her with both his hands under her arms, hoisting her in the air so that she had no leverage.

Solitaire grinned, a line of blood tracing a trickle from his split lip to his chin. With his bristling crew cut and hardened appearance, he seemed like a demented drill sergeant. "Having fun yet?"

Buffy forced herself to smile, to conceal how much pain his crushing grip was causing her. "You sure know how to show a girl a good time." She held the smile long enough to slam her knee into his chin.

Roaring, he carried her across the room and threw her bodily down on a display case. Glass crashed beneath her and her head struck a metal support, momentarily stunning her. Solitaire picked her up out of the debris and hurled her headfirst toward the floor. She had enough presence of mind to roll, absorbing the impact with her shoulder. But she came up short, striking the opposite wall awkwardly.

Her mother uttered a muffled shout through her gag. Buffy looked up as Solitaire removed a broadsword from its wall mount. He gripped it in two hands and was about to drive it through her, impaling her on the floor. She rolled away at the last moment, feeling the sharp metal tear the sleeve of her shirt, nicking her flesh before it drove an inch deep into the hardwood floor. She jumped up and lashed out with a kick that split the pinned sword in half.

Solitaire aimed for her face with the truncated end of

the broadsword. She ducked to the side and the blade rammed into the plaster of the wall. Buffy pulled a hefty V-shaped shield from a bracket and bashed it over his head. He staggered backward, losing his grip on the pommel of the broadsword. Buffy followed up with another two-handed blow with the shield, and another, forcing him ever backward. She hooked a foot behind his ankle and shoved the shield into him, using the shattered display cases as a fulcrum. Solitaire spun head over heels, flipping over the case and falling with a rain of shattered glass and broken artifacts.

Buffy spotted her stake and had it in her hand even as Solitaire climbed to his feet, glass tinkling all around him, looking a little wobbly. His face was cut in many places and it no longer looked completely human. He was sporting a vampface and overly long fangs. They were unlike those of any vampire she had ever seen or staked, even longer and more oddly shaped than the Master's. Buffy wondered briefly if the expression long in the tooth had come from such creatures as Solitaire. But only briefly. She grabbed him by the top of his vest with her left hand, her right hand poised over his heart, clutching the stake with white knuckles. "When you get back to hell," Buffy said, "tell them the Slayer sent you."

She drove the stake into his chest, deep enough to puncture his ancient, withered heart. Solitaire just laughed.

Buffy was taken aback. First the invulnerability to the sun, then the apparent immunity to the uninvite spell, and now he was proof against stakes. "How?"

Solitaire grabbed her shoulders in his strong hands.

"I'll tell you a little secret," he whispered in her ear. "I'm not a vampire. I just play one on TV."

Buffy swung her arms up, then out, breaking free of his grip. She backed up a step or two, but maintained a defensive posture as she watched him tug the stake out of his chest. Dark green blood oozed from the wound.

"Actually you weren't even close to my heart. Rather, hearts, I should say. I have six, one on top of the other, along my spine."

"What are you?"

"You've only seen my partial transformation," Solitaire commented. She watched as his skin became green and pebbly, his head overly large. He had fangs top and bottom. The bristly hair was replaced by spiky quills. At the sides of his head, horns appeared and grew long enough to make a bull envious. "I'm something of a demon myself," he said. "Personally, I can't stand vampires. Disgusting half-breeds!"

It all made sense, of course. Angel had never believed in the Day Walker legend and rightly so. A true vampire could not survive the direct rays of the sun. The Day Walker was a myth, a myth created by a demon masquerading as an invulnerable vampire to strike fear into their unbeating hearts. Solitaire might not have the weaknesses of a vampire, but that didn't mean he was invulnerable. *He's a demon. And demons die.* She remembered something else Angel had said, about Solitaire being a warrior caught up in his pride, an oversized ego.

"You're nothing but a coward and a fraud," Buffy taunted.

"That's harsh," Solitaire replied. He took a menacing

step toward her and she backed up an equal distance. "But now that you know you can't stake me, why not be a good little girl and die?"

"You hide behind a disguise. You attack your opponents when they are most vulnerable because you know you would lose a fair fight." She pointed to her mother. "You take hostages. If anyone is unworthy, it's you!"

"How dare you!" Solitaire's green skin darkened and his eyes smoldered red, as if hot coals had been banked behind them. He roared and charged her, using his extra weight to bull her backward. Backhand after forehand landed on her face. She was dizzy and felt her legs go rubbery. *As battle tactics go, insulting him was probably a bad idea.*

The demon wrapped a clawed hand around her neck, still holding her stake in his other hand. "I believe your own heart is conveniently front and center," he said. "How's that for irony? A Slayer impaled on her own wooden stake." He raised the stake above her heart.

Joyce Summers had finally worked her gag free. Her voice hoarse, she nonetheless screamed, "Buffy!"

Her mother's voice brought Buffy back into focus. She slammed her heel down on Solitaire's instep. The blow caused him to loosen his hold. It was enough. Buffy curled her fist and struck Solitaire hard in the throat. If he'd had an Adam's apple, she would have smashed it and crushed his windpipe. Instead he became enraged and doubled over, but not in pain. He charged her, intending to impale her on his prodigious horns. She caught the horns in her hands and held on, thinking they might be his weakness, if she could rip them from his head. But he raised his head, lifting her off her feet and using her body as a battering ram. Her body slammed into the gallery door, plate glass crashing behind her. As Solitaire backed up, she lost her grip on his horns and fell into a pile of broken glass, too tired to stand, too weak to fight. Mostly she was stunned by how quickly the tide of the battle had turned against her.

"Oh, Buffy," her mother cried from across the gallery.

Buffy looked up at Solitaire. He had walked away for some reason and now he was returning, flicking something between his fingers. The playing card, she realized.

"Game over, Slayer," he said.

Buffy tried to stand, slipped and cut her forearm on a shard of glass.

Solitaire laughed. "Don't trouble yourself. I can wring your neck right where you sit. If it's any comfort, you were a worthy opponent, Buffy the Slayer."

CHAPTER 14

Oz almost thought he was hallucinating when the Vyxn van's headlights winked on. He hadn't seen the band climb into the van nor had Cordelia come out to warn them. Nevertheless, the van was pulling out of its parking space. "Showtime," Oz said and turned the key in the ignition. The starter ground several times but refused to turn over. "C'mon . . ."

"But where's Cordelia?" Giles said, craning his head out the open window. Young men were stumbling out of the Bronze, looking tired and confused.

"Don't know, but we can't wait— There she is!"

Cordelia pushed her way through the first wave of guys to exit the Bronze. The Vyxn van turned right, its headlights sweeping across their windshield, momentarily blinding them.

Cordelia grabbed the side door of Oz's van and slid it open. "Sorry," she said, out of breath. "Some jerk spilled soda all over my dress so I had to—"

"Cordelia, you must follow us in your car and—"

"Hey, where's Buffy?"

The van's engine finally turned over, then roared as Oz tapped the accelerator. "Guys, we're gonna lose them!"

"Cordelia, there's no time to explain," Giles said. "Follow us in your car. Once we find the ghouls' lair, come back here and wait for Buffy."

Cordelia stepped down outside the van. "Follow, find, come back and wait. Hey, no problem."

As she ran toward her red sports car, parked several yards behind the van, Angel slid the side door shut and Oz drove out of the parking lot.

In a state of near panic, Oz thought he'd lost sight of Vyxn's van. Not that Giles or Angel would have noticed his unease. Unless they looked at his eyes. They darted left to right and back again, checked side- and rearview mirrors, looked in every conceivable direction as he sought any sign of Vyxn's dark van. For a few agonizing minutes, he was sure that they'd lost the ghouls and with them, any chance of ever finding Willow alive.

Fortunately, Angel moved forward and leaned over the front seat, his night-adapted vampire eyes scanning rapidly in all directions. Finally, he pointed to the right. "There," he said. "Four traffic lights down. About to turn left."

Oz looked for a long moment before the van registered and he let out a breath he hadn't known he was holding. As he sped up to make it through a yellow light,

Oz glanced in the sideview mirror and noticed Cordelia's sports car dart through the intersection just as the light turned red. With a burst of speed, she caught up to him and stayed right on top of his rear bumper.

Angel craned his neck to look in the direction Buffy had gone. He couldn't help feeling he should be in Giles's car with her, but knew she couldn't risk her mother's life. Still, if anything happened to her, he'd never be able to forgive himself. And for an immortal vampire, *never* could be a long time, an unbearably long time. Unless he decided to do some day-walking of his own. *Take care of yourself, Buffy,* Angel thought. *I can't—I won't go on without you.*

Buffy's entire plan of attack against Solitaire had been flawed from the beginning. Solitaire's manufactured history as a day-walking vampire had been a ruse to strike fear into real vampires. And to fool opponents. She had fought him to the point of exhaustion, just to get into position to stake him. *And I did stake him. For all the good it did.*

Even though all her muscles were quivering at or near exhaustion, Buffy struggled to rise, the shattered pieces of plate glass crunching beneath her. Though she was cut in a dozen places and bruised in a dozen more, she'd inflicted as much, if not more, damage to the demon. Unfortunately, he was still standing while she was not.

Solitaire couldn't resist gloating. "Just had a marvelous idea," he said. "Instead of the mother watching her daughter die, why not the other way around? Have the Slayer watch her own mother die moments before her own crushing defeat. A much sweeter victory for me. Don't you agree, Slayer?"

Solitaire lifted a pitted rondel dagger from a wall display and tapped his finger against the point. Hundreds of years old, it was still lethal. He started to turn toward Joyce Summers, who gasped when she realized his intent.

It's now or never, Buffy realized. She gritted her teeth and sprang to her feet. "Wait!"

Solitaire faced her again, smug, as if he expected her to beg. "Wait. For what?"

"This," she said and lashed out with a jagged piece of glass she'd palmed, slicing a deep line across his chest drawing more of his dark green blood.

It startled him more than anything, but only for a moment. He lashed out with the dagger and it was all she could do to avoid having her face parted down the middle. The glinting ·blade whistled millimeters from her nose. While she was still off-balance, Solitaire stepped forward and slammed his palm in her face, shoving her head back hard against the metal doorframe. With the impact, stars exploded inside her skull and she dropped again to the floor. For a moment or two, she was too dazed to move. Her muscles simply refused to respond.

"Now, where were we?" Solitaire said as he turned away and walked toward Buffy's mother again.

The immediate threat to her mother delivered a jolt of adrenaline. Buffy started to climb to her feet again, this time reaching out for support. Her fingers closed around the cool shaft of the double-headed ax supported by the crossed gauntlets of the suit of armor beside the door.

She shook off her exhaustion and hoisted the ax up in her arms, like a baseball bat. "Solitaire!"

"Unbelievable," Solitaire said, stopping and turning back to her. "A little spunk left?"

She stepped into the swing and the blur of gleaming metal whistled through the air. At first she thought she'd completely missed him. The startled expression on his face remained frozen there for a second, and another as he slowly toppled forward. Or at least his body toppled forward. The two curved horns on his head were heavily weighted to the rear of his skull. His head slid smoothly backward, rolling down his falling back and bouncing off his heavily muscled calf to wobble around the exhibition room in a half circle, coming to rest under one of the intact display cases. His body hit the floor with a dull thud, the rondel dagger flying free of nerveless fingers to land at Buffy's feet.

"In these tense situations, it's real important to keep your head," Buffy said to no one in particular. Her mother certainly wasn't listening. She just stared, jaw hanging in shock and disbelief.

As Buffy crouched to pick up the dagger, she heard a bubbling sound coming from Solitaire's body. Within his black clothing and red vest, his green flesh was quickly losing its consistency, like butter melting in a hot saucepan. Solid turned to liquid with a little noxious vapor in the mix. Soon only a pool of green goo remained of his flesh. When the clothing collapsed, a handful of playing cards spilled out of a vest pocket. Farther away, Solitaire's head had dissolved into another slimy mess. All that was left of his horns were twin mounds of black ash.

Buffy hurried to her mother's side, cutting the ropes that bound her arms and legs, then slicing the fallen gag free of her neck. She hugged her mother fiercely. "You okay, Mom?"

"I'm fine, dear," she said. "But you—?"

"Ditto on the fine," Buffy said. She glanced at the puddle of goo and shook her head. "He thought by attacking my family and my friends that he'd gain an advantage over me. That just made me fight all the harder."

"Guess he underestimated you."

"Last mistake he'll ever make," Buffy said. "Mom, I gotta go. Willow and Xander need—"

"No need to explain, Buffy."

"You're sure you're okay?"

"Fine. Now go!"

"Love you, Mom," Buffy called as she ran for the shattered door.

"Love you, too," Joyce said. "And be careful!"

But Buffy was already gone.

"Ouch!" Xander shouted. "I think I broke a toe— make that *toes.*"

Both his shoes and trousers were coated in plaster dust and bits of lath. He'd been kicking large holes in the wall in an effort to get his hands behind the large board that held their chain hooks. Even though Willow told him she believed the board was secured to beams, he thought it was worth a try. Instead of arguing—since she had no better idea of her own—she had moved as far away as her neck chain would allow. Still, the pluming plaster dust had been enough to give her fits of coughing.

"What I wouldn't give for a sledgehammer right now," Xander said. He plopped down on the floor and gently tugged his shoe free of his injured foot.

"As long as you're wishing," Willow suggested, "why not just wish for a pair of bolt cutters?"

"And take the easy way out?" Xander quipped, but was unable to maintain a light-hearted tone. Only one thing weighed heavily on his mind. "We're running out of time, aren't we?"

"Yep," Willow said, her voice seeming frightened and alone in the darkness.

"Damn it all!" Xander said and threw his torn shoe, which slammed against the splintered doorframe. The shoe rebounded off the door and came flying back, nearly striking his head. "Okay, I'm enrolling in that anger management class . . . if we ever get out of here." But the shoe's impact caused the door to swing open, away from the damaged latch, with a prolonged creaking of its old hinges.

"At least you got the door open," Willow said, offering faint encouragement.

"It was already broken." Besides, the stench of rotting meat was that much stronger with the door open.

"Oh, right."

"Hey, look," Xander said, pointing at the table in the other room. "Do you see it?"

"A table?"

"On *top* of the table. Shining." Xander stood again, leaning forward to get a better look. "Will, that's—it's the key ring with keys for our collars. They left the keys right out there."

"Why not?" Willow said. "With us chained in here."

"If I had a rope I could tie it around a hunk of this plaster and go fishing for the keys," he said. "Saw it in an old western movie. Or could have been an episode of the 'Brady Bunch.'"

"Rope," Willow said. "That would be the thing we keep on a shelf with the sledgehammer and bolt cutters."

Xander sighed. "Yep, I got a serious case of the 'if only's.'"

"No, wait!" Willow said. "I have an idea. I've been practicing. If it's not too heavy, I might be able to—"

"What? Willow, it sounds like you have the makings of a plan in that gorgeous head of yours."

"Thanks," Willow said, "but I need quiet."

"Quiet?"

"I've been practicing. Levitating small objects. Seems like part of my whole Wicca awakening."

"Objects?"

"Well, pencils mostly," she explained. "But it requires concentration and right now I'm tired and hungry and have a really nasty plaster-dust headache."

"Not to mention the prospect of becoming a flesh-eating ghoul by midnight."

"Thanks for reminding me."

"Little motivation couldn't hurt," Xander said. "And if we don't get out of here soon, they're gonna be calling me fillet o' Xander."

"Okay, okay, be quiet now."

Xander watched as Willow's brow furrowed in concentration, her gaze locked on the key ring. One large, bracelet-sized ring had several long, antiquated keys dangling from it. She would only have to move it twelve, maybe fifteen feet to bring it within reach. Looking back and forth from Willow to the key ring, Xander waited and hoped for some sign that Willow might be able to succeed. At first he simply saw the strain of effort in Willow's face, in her clenched jaw and furrowed brow, in her extended arms, reaching hands and trembling fingers, but the key ring remained motionless. Until finally, the large ring quivered, lifted and leaned toward her, as if tugged by a magnet. But it wasn't magnetic force, it was telekinetic—and it was working!

"That's it, Will!"

Willow released an explosive breath. "No good."

"Sorry," Xander said. "I—"

"No, it's okay," Willow explained. "I was doing it wrong."

"It moved, Will. I saw it."

"Can't hold my breath while I do this," Willow said. "Takes too long. Can't maintain concentration that way. Okay, here goes." She began again, breathing steadily, as she stretched her hand toward the key ring and achieved results in less time than before. The large key ring twitched again, but if Xander had been expecting the key ring to rise into the air and float toward them, he was no less impressed when it began to scrape along the wooden tabletop. All those keys had to be much heavier than a pencil and in Willow's exhausted condition dragging them was probably the best she could manage. Not that it mattered. All she needed to do was bring the key ring within arm's reach any way she could.

Perspiration had appeared on Willow's furrowed brow, while droplets of sweat that trickled down her face formed tracks in the light coating of plaster dust on her cheek and neck. Still, her gaze remained fixed on the keys. Xander's own nose itched from the dust, but he resisted scratching it, worried the slight movement would jar Willow out of her self-imposed trance.

When the keys dropped off the table and struck the floor in a metallic clatter, she let out a sharp gasp. With the break in her concentration, she cast a quick glance at Xander, who gave a smile and nod of encouragement. After a brief respite, just enough time to take a deep breath and try to work the kink out of her neck, Willow resumed her effort.

Soon the tendons in her outstretched hands quivered like high tension wires and the trembling of her fingers intensified. Inch by inch, the keys scraped along the floor, pulled by the large ring that seemed the sole focus of her concentration. She was pulling the ring. The keys just came along for the ride.

As her body stretched forward her chain became taut, and the iron collar bit into her neck. Xander thought he could make out a trickle of blood that would probably require a tetanus shot. Just a few feet more and she would have the keys. They would be free and the nightmare would end.

Oz switched off his headlights as soon as the Vyxn van took a right turn onto what appeared to be a private access dirt road. Fortunately, Cordelia was paying attention and likewise extinguished her own headlights. Otherwise, away from the main flow of traffic, it would be too obvious to the ghouls that they were being followed. Even with his headlights off, Oz stayed back a considerable distance. The dirt road was uneven and cratered with nasty potholes, forcing him to slow down. If the Scooby Gang's luck held, the ghouls would have all their attention on the hazards of the road and not on the dark blue van a hundred yards behind them. In addition to the natural cover of night, Cordelia's flashy red Cirrus would be shielded behind Oz's bulkier van.

Beyond the trees, the road followed the steady incline of a hill, terminating beside an abandoned and probably condemned two-story house with a peaked roof. Ominously dark in silhouette against the skyline of the modest hill, the house was fronted by a field of wild grass interspersed with patches of rampant weeds.

Something about the house triggered a memory in Oz. "No," he whispered in sudden realization, involuntarily hitting his brake.

Giles looked at him. "What?"

"That's the Gatton place."

"Afraid I'm unfamiliar with— Gatton, you say?"

"Late eighties," Oz said. "Old man Gatton hung his wife, two kids in the attic, shot himself." *And Willow's in there! She has to be in there.*

"Judging by its state of disrepair, I'd say it's been unoccupied ever since."

"Rumor says it's haunted."

"Well—given our location over the Hellmouth—I suppose that's entirely possible."

"We may not find any ghosts," Angel said from the back. "But it's home to a pack of ghouls right now."

The Vyxn van had parked on the weed-strewn gravel driveway beside the house. Their lights winked off a moment before the doors opened and four wild-haired figures climbed out of the van.

"Let's park here," Giles said. "We're obscured by the trees and less likely to draw their attention."

Oz nodded. A glance in the rearview mirror showed Cordelia's Cirrus backing up into a three-point turn. She risked a broken axle or worse if she attempted to navigate the dirt road in reverse. *She'll bring Buffy, assuming Buffy has finished with Solitaire by now. And no guarantee of that.* "What now?" Oz asked. With every fiber of his being he wanted to charge the house, kick down the door and get Willow out of there. Then again, he had to admit to himself he probably wasn't thinking rationally at the moment.

"We surround the house," Angel said. "Attack from all sides."

"We need to approach this situation with some caution," Giles warned. "Three of us against four bloodthirsty ghouls who possess a supernatural ability to bend us to their will."

"Their singing has no effect on me," Angel pointed out.

"Interesting, that," Giles remarked. "I suppose the flesh of the undead has no appeal to ghouls and therefore—"

"Giles!" Oz interrupted.

"Oh, yes, sorry. As I was saying, three against four,

while I only have the use of one arm and you, Angel, are still recovering from—"

"Don't worry about me," Angel said. "I'm eighty-five—make that ninety percent."

"If Oz and I succumb to their . . . spell, that would make the odds four against one," Giles said. "Possibly six against one if they can turn us against you."

"So what are you suggesting?" Oz asked. "We can't just wait! Not while Willow—and Xander—could be in there."

"I'm not suggesting we wait," Giles said. "Just that we should not charge in unprepared." Giles reached into one of the pockets of his tweed jacket. It lay draped over the seat of the van, as he'd been unable to slip it on comfortably over the cast on his arm. "That's why I brought these," he said as he produced several small packages.

"Earplugs," Oz said, reading the label.

While Ulysses's men had stuffed wax in their ears to navigate past the sirens, the Scooby Gang would rely on cushioned earplugs. "They may not be completely effective," Giles explained. "So we must not become careless."

"Gotcha," Oz said. He took a package, ripped it open then rolled the cylindrical plugs between his fingers until they were narrow enough to push into his ear canal. Almost immediately they began to expand. "Talk to me."

"Can you hear me?" Giles said in a normal speaking voice.

"Yes, but you're muffled," Oz said. "Even my own voice sounds strange."

"That's natural," Giles said. "Angel, I suggest you use a pair as well."

"But I'm not aff—"

"They've only been trying to control humans," Giles said. "They may have other . . . pitches or frequencies or whatever to control vampires. Best to be safe." Angel nodded and took a package from Giles.

Oz removed his own earplugs temporarily and asked, "So, what's the plan?"

"Ideally, Buffy would lead the attack," Giles replied. To forestall Oz's interruption, Giles held up a hand. "However, we can't know how long she'll be . . . otherwise occupied. So it's up to us." He cleared his throat. "If Willow and Xander are in the house, we need to attack decisively, while we have the element of surprise."

"I'll scout the house for entry points," Angel said.

"Very good," Giles said.

Angel eased open the side door and slipped into the night. Silently, Giles and Oz watched his progress, a low darting black shape in his long duster, flowing through the tall weeds and grass. Now and then they lost sight of him, only to see him reappear as he looped around the far side of the house. Staying low, close to the wall of the Gatton house, he slipped around the back.

The seconds ticked by.

As she approached the intersection where she needed to turn left to return to the Bronze, Buffy spotted Cordelia's red sports car racing up the cross street. *She knows where the ghouls live!* Buffy's glance returned to the intersection and saw her green turn arrow had already changed from yellow to red with a line of traffic ready to roll from the opposite direction.

"Sorry, Giles," she said as she floored the accelerator

of his car and swerved hard to the left, a full fifty yards before the intersection. As the Citroën rumbled over the median strip, her head bounced painfully against the roof. She angled in front of the opposing lanes of traffic well ahead of the oncoming cars and a potential head-on collision, but grimaced at the squeal of the car's dipping undercarriage as it scraped against the wide driveway of the corner gas station. She zipped between a massive display of shrink-wrapped soda cases and a startled gas station attendant, who dropped his squeegee and dove across the hood of a car he'd been filling with premium.

Cutting across the corner of the gas station lot, she drove out onto the cross street, headed in the wrong direction until she jumped another median strip with a spray of sparks. As soon as she spotted Cordelia's red car, just three blocks ahead, she started pounding on the horn and flashing her headlights, a display that should catch even Cordelia's attention.

Willow strained to reach the key ring as it inched ever closer to her fingertips. Xander was taller and would have had a long enough reach to grab the keys already, except his hands were still chained behind him. It was up to her, completely. The large ring wavered in the air and lurched another inch closer, dragging the long keys behind it. She almost moaned with the effort. Her concentration was so focused she was barely aware of Xander urging her on . . . or the reason for his sudden agitation.

The other voices, coming from outside, never registered.

But the door to the outer room, to the outside world, creaked and she knew it was almost too late. Her fingers brushed against the ring but were quivering so much she missed on the first grab.

Someone yelled, "The door's open!"

"The keys!"

Willow gasped as her index and middle finger curled around the large ring. "Got it!" She yanked the key ring——as a foot slammed down on the keys.

"Not thinking of leaving us, were you?" Lupa asked, tugging the keys from Willow's trembling hand.

Xander caught Willow's pained expression as she scrambled back against the wall. "You did your best, Will." She nodded but felt dejected nonetheless. *Almost isn't good enough.*

Lupa took in the battered wall, the proliferation of plaster dust. "Certainly have made a mess of the place, haven't you. Look, I admit we have been less than perfect hosts, but things are just about to get interesting."

"Anyone notice if we were followed?" Lupa asked the other ghouls.

"Thought I saw taillights at the end of the road," Rave replied.

Lupa looked to the others, but both shook their heads. They hadn't noticed anything. "Let's assume the encore is on, then. Nash, why don't you make sure everything is ready for our special guest. Including our little Slayer surprise."

"Ghoul's motto, I say. Always be prepared."

Nash slipped into the outer room, leaving the door open wide enough for Willow to watch as the ghoul drummer lit and turned up the wick of the oil lamp, filling the outer room with golden light. Next she opened a wooden chest and reached inside for some metal contraption.

Lupa turned to her lead guitarist. "Rave, let's begin the Rite of Initiation."

Rave nodded, left the room for a few moments, then returned with an ancient metal chalice and a jeweled dagger, in the bronze hilt of which had been carved human bodies twisted in torment. She'd left the door open wide enough to provide some light, but not wide enough for Willow to watch Nash as she assembled the "Slayer surprise" in the outer room. Rave handed Lupa the dagger, then placed the chalice in the center of the floor.

"Hold his hands," Lupa said to Carnie and Rave. "We'll begin."

All three ghouls in the room with Willow and Xander transformed into their ghoulish aspects, their true appearances, with mottled green skin, sharp rows of gnarled teeth, nasty claws twitching at the end of powerful arms. Once again, Willow was unnerved by their multiple rows of sharp teeth. She could imagine tendrils of rotting flesh still caught between all those fangs, which would certainly account for their foul breath.

The two ghouls positioned themselves on either side of Xander and gripped his arms—still locked behind his back—and twisted his hands so his palms faced up. Though he struggled in their grip, Xander was unable to pull free, so he began to kick at Lupa and her ceremonial dagger.

"Enough of this, Lupa," Rave said. "Compel him!"

The leader of the ghouls sighed. "Oh, very well. Though it's so much sweeter when they put up a little fight." Lupa stared into Xander's panic-stricken eyes. As she spoke, her voice was warm and soothing, a blanket wrapped around his fear, an aural drug to lull him into a state of complacency. "Xander, you must stand perfectly still. Nod if you understand."

Willow didn't understand how it worked, but it certainly seemed effective. Xander became still, relaxed even. His eyes became unfocused, staring off into space, as if he were completely unconcerned with what was about to happen to him. Slowly, to Willow's horror, he nodded.

"Good," Lupa said. "Now let's continue."

Carnie and Rave held his palms in position again.

"Stop it!" Willow shouted, jumping up and grabbing one of Carnie's arms with her manacled hands.

Carnie released Xander long enough to drive an elbow into Willow's stomach, then backhanded her with enough force to drive her against the wall, where she stumbled and fell with a rattle of chains. "It's impolite to interrupt, little girl," Carnie said.

Lupa made two quick slashes across Xander's palms.

His eyes abruptly alert, Xander cried out in pain. "I gotta say, that smarts."

Carnie and Rave positioned his hands over the chalice Lupa had picked up off of the floor, letting his blood stream into it. Xander pulled against the two ghouls holding him. Again, Lupa commanded, "Stand still."

Xander nodded.

Rave finished collecting blood. She poured it slowly on the floor, forming a circle. After she set aside the chalice, she unlocked Xander's collar, freeing him from the wall chain. Next she unfastened and removed his manacles. "Stand in the circle, Xander."

Xander walked stiffly, as if fighting the overwhelming impulse to do exactly as she said—but obeying nonetheless. When he reached the center of the circle, he stopped and waited.

"Xander?" Willow said. "You're free! Run!"

Lupa laughed. "You're not a ghoul yet, Willow. But someday men *will* run when you tell them."

"I have no intention of becoming a ghoul," Willow said, lifting her chin in defiance.

"We don't stand on ceremony," Lupa said. "Well, not much. All that remains is for you to eat of his living flesh and after about a fortnight of fevers, nausea and hallucinations, the transformation will be complete. You'll be one of us."

"It's not as bad as all that," Carnie assured her. "Go on, we'll have a blast."

Nash returned to the room. "So we're dressing for the occasion," she said and transformed into her ghoulish aspect as well. She turned to Lupa. "All ready for the Slayer."

"Good," Lupa said. "If I close my eyes, I can almost taste her still-beating heart."

"All right for you," Nash said. "But what about the rest of us? We'd like a taste, wouldn't we, ghouls?" Rave and Carnie remained silent, refused to make eye contact with her. "C'mon now, I'm not the only one's thought about taking a nibble. Enough for all, I say. Why should you be the only one—?"

In a flash, Lupa had the bloodied point of the ceremonial dagger pressed under Nash's chin. A single upward thrust of the long blade and Lupa would impale Nash's mouth and skewer her brain. "You're forgetting, Nash. The ceremony is explicit. Slayer's heart must be devoured whole. Only the leader may reap the strength of ten ghouls and be made invulnerable for a hundred years. The question is, Nash—and recall that poor Viola answered this very same question incorrectly—are you challenging me for leadership of the troupe?" Nash's eyes were wide with fright as she shook her head. "So nice to reach consensus," Lupa quipped. She still held the dagger to the drummer's throat. "Any questions, Nash?"

The spiked collar on the drummer's neck bobbed as she swallowed hard. She shook her head. "Miss anything, did I?"

Finally Lupa released Nash. The drummer casually rubbed the nick on her flesh and found a drop of green blood there.

"Willow was just about to join us," Lupa told her.

"Try it," Nash encouraged, apparently hoping to make amends. "You'll *really* like it."

Lupa held up the jeweled dagger, which was still streaked with Xander's blood. "Just tell me where to cut. Slice of the thigh? Abdomen? Upper arm?"

"You're crazy," Willow whispered. "You're all crazy."

"She's just not hungry enough yet," Carnie remarked.

"I'd rather starve to death!"

"Unfortunately, we can't wait that long," Lupa said. "All our ceremonies take place under the dark of the new moon."

"Tough cookies," Willow said, crossing her arms over

her chest. Just mentioning the word *cookies* set her stomach to a new fit of grumbling, despite the lingering soreness from Carnie's attack. Willow was awfully hungry . . . but would never be *that* hungry.

"We're wasting time," Rave said.

"Let's just force feed her," Nash said, her wide grin exposing about thirty yellowed teeth, saliva running between them in stringy rivulets.

"You wouldn't!" Willow said, then caught herself. "What am I thinking? Of course you *would*."

"Forcing is hit or miss," Lupa admitted. "We could prepare a ghoul nectar from special bodily secretions, but it takes time to prepare and even more time to kick in and . . . loosen your inhibitions. And we're certainly not waiting around another month for you to become sufficiently starved to eat what you're offered. So, how about a deal? Take a few bites of your pal here. I'll even *convince* him not to feel much pain, if you'd like. Fog his memory on just who took a few bites out of him. Then we'll set him free, let him live."

"You would let him go?" Willow asked.

Lupa smiled, taking special care not to expose too many of her daggerlike teeth. "Sure. Why not? The important thing is when we next hit the road, you'll have a healthy green glow and we'll have a brand-new keyboard player."

"Keyboard player," Willow repeated, numb.

"No way we're letting you stand around slapping a tambourine," Carnie joked.

Willow bit her lip, desperately trying to think of a way out of the mess she found herself in. Lupa was lying to her. Of that, she had no doubt. The ghouls would never free Xander. He knew all about their cover as a band. Even if she believed Lupa, Willow could never eat Xander's flesh. The idea was too hideous to consider for even one moment. Yet Xander was no longer chained and it occurred to Willow that maybe she could save Xander, even if it meant sacrificing herself.

"This is a limited time offer," Lupa said. "What's it gonna be, Willow?"

Xander turned his head to her with what looked like extraordinary effort. He whispered harshly, "Don't do it, Willow!"

Lupa hissed at him, baring all her many and varied fangs. "Be quiet, you worthless piece of flesh." But her voice was impatient and lacked the sing-song rhythm to compel him. Instead, she slapped him across the face. "This grows tiresome," Lupa said to Willow, her eyes glowing a feral yellow in the gloom. "Choose to become one of us or I kill you both now!"

"Okay—okay!" Willow said. "But if I do this, I should be the one to cut him." She took a deep breath and reached out her manacled hands. "Give me the dagger."

CHAPTER 15

Through gaps in the boarded-up windows at the front of the Gatton house, light spilled out onto the overgrown lawn, yet the house remained a mystery. Angel had not reappeared since slipping around back, and Oz was beginning to wonder if something had happened to him. "This is taking too long," Oz remarked, his hands tight on a crowbar he'd removed from the long toolbox in the back of the van. "Where's Angel?"

Balancing a loaded crossbow on the dashboard, Giles was about to respond when he felt the van dip slightly under added weight. Worried they had been caught unawares, Giles spun around in his seat, sighting along the crossbow, finger about to squeeze on the trigger.

"Whoa!" Angel called, palms up, facing the Watcher. "On your side, remember?"

"Quite right," Giles said calmly, but his heart was racing. He'd nearly staked their best chance of rescuing Willow and Xander.

"Willow's in there," Oz said, more statement than question. "She's in there, right?"

Angel nodded. "They're both in there. But something's going down. Some ceremony. We don't have much time."

Giles was relieved—incredibly relieved—yet worried at the same time. Willow and Xander were still alive, but far from safe at the moment. "Tell us," Giles said.

"On the side of the house, I found a set of double doors leading down into the basement. Padlocked, but the wood was so rotted I just ripped the lock plate off. Giles, you and Oz enter that way. They might have somebody watching the back door, but they probably won't be expecting an attack from within the house. I'll give you a couple minutes to get into position."

"What about you?" Oz asked.

"I'm immune to their power, so I'll go in loud, right through the front door. A direct assault to distract them. Then you two make your move. We'll outflank them. Take them out before they know what hit them."

"Wait a minute," Giles said. "Will you be able to enter the house—uninvited, that is?"

"Humans abandoned that house long ago," Angel said. "I won't have a problem."

"Sounds like a plan," Oz said.

"Earplugs, everyone," Giles cautioned. All three of them put in their earplugs. "One other thing." Ignoring the odd quality of his own voice, Giles reached into a burlap bag, removed a long gleaming blade and handed it to Angel.

"A scimitar?" Angel asked. He tested the weight and balance in his hands.

Giles nodded. "Ghouls have their roots in Arabic folklore. It's possible an Arabian blade will prove more effective against them than traditional weapons."

"Let's move," Oz said.

Giles could not fault the young man's urgency. Each carrying a weapon, they exited the van, abandoned the concealment of the trees and crept along the wide expanse of tall grass. Angel tapped Giles on the shoulder and pointed toward the front of the house and held up two fingers. Giles nodded, took Oz's arm and pointed toward the side of the house. Angel would give them two minutes to get inside the house. The next time Giles glanced back, Angel had already slipped away in the tall grass, getting into position for a frontal assault. Giles hurried to catch up to Oz.

They found the aboveground doors leading down into the basement, a wedge-shape pressed against the side of the house. Oz lifted the outer door up in a slow, steady motion to avoid any creaking that might give away their position. He started down the concrete flight of stairs and made a hand motion of turning a doorknob, indicating another door at the base of the stairs. Then he lifted the crowbar, signaling his intent to break and enter. Oz took another step down, then paused, his eyes wide. Even as he pointed with the crowbar, Giles was turning toward the front of the house.

In the distance, a fleeting glimpse of red moving low

through the grass, but closer still, running low toward him in black cargo pants and a spaghetti strap top, with a flash of blond hair . . .

"Buffy . . ." he whispered, relieved. He tugged out one earplug. "I thought you'd never get here."

"Better late than dead," Buffy said. She made no mention of her bloody ear or the cuts and scratches on her arms. Giles noticed she had stopped at the van long enough to grab another crossbow from their supply of weapons.

"So . . . Solitaire—?"

"Lost his head," she replied. "But my mom's fine."

Cordelia burst out of the grass and weeds, stumbling slightly on the gravel before recovering her balance. Still slightly out of breath, she whispered, "Yuck—the lawn that time forgot."

Buffy caught Giles's good arm, the one clutching his own crossbow. "Giles, what's the sitch? And where's Angel?"

Lupa flipped the knife in her hand and offered it hilt-first to Willow. "Just remember," she said, "you're still in chains and the four of us are much stronger than you."

"I know," Willow replied as meekly as she could.

Lupa touched Xander's shoulder. "Xander," she said in a warm, melodic voice. "You will not resist. Understood?" He nodded, his gaze again unfocused. Lupa looked down at Willow, sitting just outside Xander's circle of blood. "Begin," she said.

Willow gripped the knife in her hand, point down.

Xander just stared straight ahead. With only one shoe on, he even looked a little comical. *His foot's probably still tender from kicking the wall.* "Sorry, Xander," she whispered.

"Go on," Lupa urged. "Make the slice. Just a few bites and become one of us."

Something hard struck the outer door, blasting it inward on its rusted hinges, followed by the loud, metallic *TWANG!* of a strong spring releasing and finally a loud grunt of pain. *Oh, no!* Willow thought. *Buffy?!*

"One Slayer surprise," Carnie said. "Served ice cold."

Lupa pulled the door open all the way, revealing an empty outer room. The door to the outside hung from one tortured hinge, still vibrating. Willow saw an oiled metallic contraption clamped to the table. A thin wire led up to the ceiling and down to the damaged door, but it was loose . . . the trap had been sprung. In a small voice, Willow called out, "Buffy?"

Angel waited a full two minutes, then rose from his concealment in the yard and charged the door with the scimitar in his left hand. At the last moment, he lowered his right shoulder and rammed the door, knocking it off its hinges. Even as he was switching the scimitar to his right hand, he glimpsed the quivering wire, heard the dull *twang!* of metal, the sound muffled by his plugged ears. A flash of steel and his side was on fire. He grunted in pain, stumbling back out the door and falling on his good side even as he examined the barbed steel spear that pierced his abdomen. He'd sprung a trap meant for Buffy. A trap that could have killed her. Since it had impaled him well below his heart, he would just hurt like hell for a while.

"Angel!" Buffy called, running toward him, crouched low, along the front of the house. Giles trailed behind her with his crossbow.

"I'm fine," Angel replied, his voice tight with pain. "Here!" He tossed her the scimitar, which she deftly caught in her right hand. To her concerned look, he said, "Go. I'm fine." As he was already pushing the barbed spear completely through his side, with an occasional but not unexpected grimace, she nodded and approached the front of the house. She knew he would heal. Willow and Xander had to be her first priority.

Oz had little trouble popping the basement door open with his crowbar. As it swung inward, he recoiled from the oppressive stench. Behind him, now carrying Buffy's crossbow, Cordelia doubled over and retched.

"This—this is the Gatton house, isn't it?" Cordelia asked.

Oz nodded.

"Please tell me we're not going in there," Cordelia said, her face ashen.

"Stay here if you want," Oz said. He stepped into the darkness of the basement.

"You're not leaving me out here," Cordelia whispered a moment later and ran in after him.

Oz tried to wait for his eyes to adjust to the deeper darkness in the basement, but only the edges of boxes, the curve of pipes and the blocky shape of a hot-water heater were visible. Until they turned a corner in the

L-shaped basement and saw them hanging there. Three dark shapes, hanging from the ceiling, heads lolling forward.

Oz's breath caught in his throat.

Cordelia gasped, clutching his arm. "That's them!" she whispered fiercely. "Gatton hung them down here!"

"No," Oz said. "It can't be them. He hung them in the attic."

"Attic. Basement. Does it really matter?"

"They wouldn't have left the bodies," Oz explained.

"Haunted. Ghosts. Gatton house. Is any of this sinking in?"

He reached into his pocket and removed the flashlight he'd brought with him from the van. When he flicked it on, Cordelia punched him. "You had a flashlight all this time?"

"Didn't want to give away our position."

The three hanging shapes hadn't moved at all. Oz was sure they weren't ghosts. He played the light across all three of them, what was left of them, then moved the beam away. A metal track had been attached to the wooden beam, with metal hooks—the kind used in slaughterhouses—to hold the bodies. There hadn't been much meat left on the bones or organs within them. Cordelia had seen enough. She was retching again. "The one in the middle," she gasped. "Oh, God! I think it was—it was Troy."

"I know."

At that moment they heard a loud crash upstairs, followed by another, metallic sound.

"Let's go!"

"Right behind you," Cordelia said, clutching the material of his shirt as she edged as far from the hanging corpses as she could. As Oz started up the rickety wooden staircase, Cordelia stumbled against the old railing and the wood began to split. Oz caught her, but not before the beam of his flashlight played across the last corpse in the row and the rat which was perched on its ravaged shoulder. The rat turned away from the light but Cordelia had already seen the red smear on its mouth.

Buffy ran into the house and kicked the table aside, banging against a teal refrigerator that looked like a junkyard reject. Buffy hated to think what the ghouls stored in there, especially without the benefit of electricity. The device that had injured Angel had been spring-loaded and designed to fire a single projectile. It was on the floor, completely harmless now. She took in the situation in the other room in a heartbeat, raised the scimitar before her and said, "Willow prefers kosher meals!"

Lupa seemed surprised that Buffy was uninjured. "We heard you—the spear—"

"Sorry," Buffy replied. "I like to do my own accessorizing. But you've made Angel real mad. And that goes double for me."

As if quoting from some dark scripture, Lupa said, "The ghoul who eats the still-beating heart of a Slayer will be made as strong as ten and invulnerable for a hundred years."

Buffy sighed. "Is there a blue-plate special on Slayers today?"

"I'm not picky," Rave said as she moved toward Willow. "I'll eat any old still-beating heart."

"You see, Slayer, we've been waiting for you. Actually hoping you'd pay us a visit," Lupa said. "Now drop your weapon and surrender. Or your friends die."

"Sorry," Willow said again to Xander and jabbed the point of the dagger into his sore toes.

Xander cried out in pain, hopping on his good foot. As Willow had hoped, the sudden pain was enough to wrench him out of his trance state.

Giles came through the door behind Buffy, a crossbow balanced on his cast.

"Party time," Buffy said.

Xander lurched sideways, driving Rave into the wall.

Seeing an advantage, Lupa pointed at Giles, a toothy grin flashing across her face. "You! I command you to strike down the Slayer. Now!"

Though Giles heard her words and knew the ghoul was attempting to control his mind, his earplugs blocked whatever special intonation or inflection was required for her voice to have the compelling effect. Giles's response was equally direct. "I think not." He took aim at Lupa and fired a crossbow bolt, right through Nash's eye.

Nash clutched at the shaft, then fell backward, into the other room, dead.

"I was aiming for the other one," Giles mumbled beside Buffy. "Her heart, actually."

Running footfalls sounded from the hallway to the right of the room where Willow and Xander had been held captive. Oz and Cordelia appeared a moment later. Cordelia was ashen, her crossbow aimed at the ceiling, while Oz appeared quite shaken himself, his crowbar gripped in his white-knuckled fist. *Something in the basement spooked them,* Buffy thought.

"Gang's all here," Buffy said. Only Angel was out of the mix.

As if on cue, Buffy heard the shriek and pop of nails being ripped from wood. Lupa backhanded Willow and yanked the ceremonial dagger out of her hands. She turned her attention to Buffy, feral yellow eyes aglow as saliva spilled down her chin, in anticipation of a still-beating Slayer heart, no doubt. Lupa charged, dagger held high. Behind her, Angel leapt into the captives' room—having ripped the plywood free of the windows—and tackled Rave just as she was about to sink her claws into Xander's face.

Carnie saw Oz come around the corner from the hallway and leapt like a jungle cat, claws flashing. Cordelia screamed and fired her crossbow at the redheaded ghoul. The bolt fluttered through red hair and maybe even nicked a mottled green ear as it sailed through the air. The quarrel then struck the hanging oil lamp and knocked it off its hook. The glass housing shattered on impact. From the shadows cast by the flickering light, Buffy could tell that oil had spilled out and the floor had caught on fire.

Carnie's momentum had bowled over Oz, who couldn't quite bring his crowbar into play, while Cordelia was knocked backward over a ladder-back chair.

Buffy lost track of the other battles as she launched into her own, landing a flying kick against Lupa's sternum. The impact knocked both of them off their feet. Lupa rolled into a crouch and dove at Buffy, dagger first. Buffy sidestepped and managed an awkward, backhanded swing of the scimitar. Lupa somersaulted and regained her feet, waving the dagger from side to side. The two circled each other, looking for an opening.

Giles managed to reload his crossbow with his good hand, while bracing it against his cast. He turned and fired at Lupa just as she feinted. The quarrel zipped past the back of her head and thudded into the wall.

Cordelia disentangled herself from the chair, stood and raised it over her head. Oz and Carnie wrestled over the crowbar and it looked as if Carnie, in the superior position and with her greater, ghoulish strength, was about to pry it from Oz's fingers. Cordelia took a step backward then swung the chair down, across Carnie's back.

"Oh, great—I broke a nail!" Cordelia cried out.

The chair had done more damage to Carnie, with two of its legs shattering across Carnie's back and shoulders. She reared up in pain, releasing the crowbar. Oz regained control of the crowbar and spun it ninety degrees to jab with it in such close quarters. At that moment, Buffy feinted with the scimitar, causing Lupa to leap backward out of the way. She slammed into Carnie, who lost her balance and fell on Oz, just as the tapered end of the crowbar was pointing straight up. It went through her throat and shattered her spine. Oz struggled out from under her, while Cordelia checked the damage to her manicure and groaned something about splinters in her palm. Oz pushed the ghoul's corpse away, disgusted as some of its skin sloughed off. The flesh was decomposing even as he watched.

Angel grappled with Rave, who normally wouldn't have been his equal in combat. However, he was still sporting a rather large hole through his abdomen, cour-

tesy of a barbed spear. While the injury wouldn't kill
him, recovering from it was sapping his strength to the
point that she was able to overbalance him and knock
him to the floor. She straddled him, claws digging into
his throat. Angel's hand swept out and caught Xander's
former collar and chain, still dangling from the wall.

Xander saw Angel's flailing intent and scrambled over
Nash's inert form—the crossbow bolt still jutting from
her eye—and picked up the length of chain. He looped it
around Rave's neck and yanked back until she released
Angel's throat. The vampire then reached up, grabbed
her head in his hands and twisted violently, breaking her
neck.

Xander released the chain and the ghoul's body slumped
to the floor. "We're even now, Dead Boy," he said.

Angel ignored the insult, just nodded and looked to
Buffy. She'd already been through a battle with Solitaire
and was probably not on top of her game either. As Xander unlocked Willow's collar and manacles with an old
key ring, Angel strode through the doorway into the
outer room.

Buffy was backed up against a boarded window in the
outer room as Lupa charged, dagger high. On the opposite side of the room, tongues of flame climbed up the
wall, lapping at the ceiling and emitting thick black
clouds of smoke. The house would be consumed by
flames in minutes. They had to get out.

"Buffy!" Angel shouted.

Ghoul and Slayer went through the window in a tan-
gle of limbs, plywood splitting and sailing away behind
them. In the hard fall on the gravel driveway outside the

house, Buffy lost her grip on the scimitar. She struck the ghoul twice with the back of her fist, shoved her away and rolled free of the debris. While Lupa was slow getting to her feet, Buffy was already up, trying to locate her scimitar in the darkness of the new-moon night.

"Give it up, Slayer," Lupa said, stalking toward her with the long knife. She swiped at Buffy with the blade, but Buffy easily sidestepped it.

"Look around," Buffy said. "Your ghoul pals are all dead. You would have been smart to leave my friends out of this. You really underestimated them. Then again, I don't look for many signs of intelligence in the demonic ranks."

Lupa roared, swinging the dagger back and forth, ever closer to Buffy's chest. Buffy jumped back and back again, until she banged into the passenger door of Vyxn's van. Lupa grinned and raised the dagger high over her head for a downward thrust. Buffy sidestepped at the last minute and heard the point of the blade screech against the metal door.

"It won't matter how many friends you have after I eat your living heart," Lupa shouted.

"Let me save you a trip to the orthodontist," Buffy said and leapt into a kick that smashed Lupa's mouth, shattering a couple rows of teeth.

Buffy ran toward the house, Lupa in hot pursuit, blood, teeth and spittle spilling from her battered mouth. The fire was blazing quite impressively now, casting enough light on the driveway for Buffy to spot the scimitar behind a clump of weeds. As Lupa hurled a section of plywood at her, Buffy somersaulted toward her weapon, clutching the hilt just as the board clipped her ankle, taking a layer or two of skin with it.

Buffy sprang to her feet, favoring her bruised ankle, scimitar in hand, but held backward, blade down. Acrid smoke billowed from the nearby front doorway, burning her nostrils and bringing tears to her eyes. As a result, she almost failed to see Lupa charging, dagger in hand, way too fast for Buffy to adjust her own grip. Instead, Buffy lashed out with a backhand blow, slamming the hilt of the scimitar into Lupa's forehead.

The ghoul staggered backward, disoriented.

Buffy flipped the scimitar over, raised it in a two-handed grip, stepped forward and brought it straight down through Lupa's skull. The curved blade lodged in the ghoul's collarbone. Buffy stepped back, releasing the blade as Lupa's lifeless body toppled over.

Angel leapt down from the window frame, then winced as he landed, pressing a hand to the wide circle of blood staining his white shirt.

"Our side okay?"

Angel nodded. "You?"

"Just glad I don't wear my heart on my sleeve," Buffy said, smiled and leaned against him, offering her support. "Everyone get out?"

"They went out the back door."

At that moment, Oz and Willow appeared from the side of the house. "Never doubted you were alive," Oz said.

"And I knew you'd come rescue me," Willow said.

They stopped in their tracks and exchanged the most fervent of smoochies. Buffy called out, "Willow. Oz. Spectators present."

For a moment they seemed not to notice, then Willow looked over at Buffy, a little flushed. "Oops," she said, with a mischievous grin.

Giles appeared next, followed by Cordelia, who was gamely offering her shoulder as support for Xander as he attempted to hop on his good foot, his other shoe held in his free hand. He was doing more yelping than hopping. "Oh, stop your whining," Cordelia said. "I have no idea what I ever saw in you."

"Just a crazy little thing called temporary insanity," Xander replied. "At least that's my excuse." He sat in the driveway long enough to tug his torn shoe on over his swollen foot, but left the laces undone. He glanced at Lupa's corpse, lying in the driveway not too far from where he was seated. "Oh, yes! Ghouls do spoil fast," Xander said to no one in particular, wrinkling his nose.

It was true. Buffy noticed the rank smell, like rancid meat, emanating from Lupa's bloated body, which looked as if it had been pulled from a swamp after three long weeks of decay. *Ready for composting,* she thought.

Willow looked at Cordelia, standing by herself in the night, arms crossed for warmth. "Cordelia, about Troy . . ."

"I know," Cordelia said, with a quick glance at Oz. "We stumbled upon what was left of him in the basement."

"I'm sorry," Willow said.

"Oh, well, I suppose there will be other screen tests in my future."

"A humbling display of compassion, Cordy," Xander said.

Cordelia looked at him archly. "What? That was two days ago. Haven't I mourned enough? It's not as if we were dating or anything. Besides, you really don't expect me to risk frown lines at my age."

"Of course not," Xander said.

Giles walked up to Buffy, empty crossbow dangling at his side as he looked at the burning house. "All in all, I'd say this was an unexpectedly successful outcome."

Xander said, "Is that your British librarian's way of saying 'all's well that ends well'?"

Willow frowned. "I'm thinking of becoming a vegan."

EPILOGUE

"**A**sk Buffy about her bad zones," Willow said to Giles. Buffy was beaming.

"Zones? Oh, yes, the source of your academic peril." Giles worked a ruler down under his cast and moved it about until it elicited a sigh of relief. It couldn't come off too soon for him. "From your delighted expression am I to assume they have improved?"

"You are. Commando—I mean, *Counselor* Burzak caught me in the hall this morning," Buffy said. "The two yellows and the red are now two greens and a blinking yellow."

"A blinking yellow, you say?"

"Oh, that's a good thing," Buffy explained. "Or at least a better thing. I think."

"I'm sure it is," Giles said loyally.

"I even saw Snyder walking around without his clipboard and evil charts," Buffy added.

"Very good, then," Giles said, obviously not wanting the entire explanation.

Xander said, "I'm still confused about this Solitaire guy. Not a vampire. Just a demon with a really big chip on his shoulder?"

"That is the essential gist of it," Giles said. "He perpetuated a false identity, a complete history, as it were, to at turns frighten and confound his opponents."

"Which reminds me," Buffy said. "The next time the Watcher journals don't seem to make much sense, there's probably a good reason. I almost learned the hard way."

"Yes," Giles conceded. "It would appear that in this instance, Angel's instincts about the Day Walker being a myth were well-founded."

"And Solitaire was not working with the ghouls?"

"No," Giles said. "What made you think he was?"

"You know what they say," Xander said. "Demons are a ghoul's best friend."

"Groan," Buffy said.

"Speaking of false histories," Giles said. "Willow, what did you finally decide to do about your dilemma? The term paper on the history of Sunnydale?"

"It was tearing me up," Willow said. "Whether to be honest and tell everything I know or to, basically, lie about everything. So, I . . . Well, I . . ."

"What?"

Oz grinned mysteriously and said, "She took the high road."

"The high road?" Giles said. "I'm not sure I follow."

Willow reached into her binder and removed a thick term paper. "This is what I wrote," she said and handed it to Giles.

He flipped through it with growing signs of alarm. "I see . . . the Hellmouth, the Master, the Slayer, Spike and Drusilla . . . This is . . . everything! Willow, surely you haven't given—!?"

With a wry smile, Willow withdrew another, much thinner paper from her binder and offered it to Giles.

He flipped through the pages, nodded and sighed. "Statistics, charts, population growth, industry and . . . and nothing supernatural." He looked at her. "Much better, but how—"

Willow shrugged with an impish grin. "I had to edit for length."

ABOUT THE AUTHOR

John Passarella lives in Swedesboro, New Jersey, with his wife and two sons. His coauthored debut novel, *Wither,* won the Bram Stoker Award for Best First Novel of 1999. *Wither* will soon be a feature film from Columbia Pictures.

Being an avid fan of the *Buffy the Vampire Slayer* television series, John decided the time had come to write his own Buffy novel after the *San Francisco Examiner & Chronicle* commented that *Wither* "hits the groove that makes TV's *Buffy the Vampire Slayer* such a kick."

Buffy the Vampire Slayer: Ghoul Trouble, is his second novel. Be sure to visit John at www.passarella.com or e-mail him at jack@passarella.com.

"YOU'RE DEAD.
YOU DON'T BELONG HERE."

Susannah just traveled a gazillion miles from New York to California in order to live with a bunch of stupid boys (her new stepbrothers). She hasn't even unpacked yet, she's made her mother practically cry already, and now there's a ghost sitting in her new bedroom. True, Jesse's a very attractive guy ghost, but that's not the point.

Life hasn't been easy these past sixteen years. That's because Susannah's a mediator—a contact person for just about anybody who croaks, leaving things...well, untidy. At least Jesse's not dangerous. Unlike Heather, the angry girl ghost hanging out at Susannah's new high school....

READ *SHADOWLAND*

BOOK #1 OF
THE MEDIATOR
BY JENNY CARROLL

. . . A GIRL BORN
WITHOUT THE FEAR GENE

FEARLESS™

A SERIES BY
FRANCINE PASCAL

**FROM POCKET PULSE
PUBLISHED BY POCKET BOOKS**

SPIKE AND DRU: PRETTY MAIDS ALL IN A ROW

The year is 1940.

In exchange for a powerful jewel, Spike and Drusilla agree to kill the current Slayer—and all those targeted to succeed her. If they succeed with their plans of bloodlust and power, it could mean the end of the Chosen One—all of the Chosen Ones—forever....

A *Buffy* hardcover
by Christopher Golden

Available from Pocket Books